Sabrina
The Teenage Witch®

Dream Boat

Mel Odom

Based upon the characters in Archie Comics

**And based upon the television series
Sabrina, The Teenage Witch
Created for television by Nell Scovell
Developed for television by Jonathan Schmock**

AN ARCHWAY PAPERBACK
Published by POCKET BOOKS
New York   London   Toronto   Sydney   Singapore

AN ARCHWAY PAPERBACK *Original*

An Archway Paperback published by
POCKET BOOKS, a division of Simon & Schuster, Inc.
1230 Avenue of the Americas, New York, NY 10020

ISBN: 0-7434-1812-3

First Archway Paperback printing December 2001

10 9 8 7 6 5 4 3 2 1

For information regarding special discounts for bulk purchases, please contact Simon & Schuster Special Sales at 1-800-456-6798 or business@simonandschuster.com

Printed in the U.S.A.

IL 4+

For all my nieces and nephews who wanted to see their names in a *Sabrina* book so they could tell people they really knew me

Gale Olson, Teneil Olson, Sierra Olson, Amy Eich, Heidi Siebels, Paul Siebels, Shailyn Peterson, Samantha Murray, Tom Murray, John Murray, Eric Anderson, Kayci Anderson, Julie Olson, April Olson, Candice Walburg, Wayne Walburg, Imoneta Odom, John Odom, Justin Odom

Dream Boat

Chapter 1

Someone is watching me, Sabrina Spellman thought as her skin prickled. That was how she always felt when someone was watching her, but usually the experience wasn't so creepy. The certainty sent a cold chill down her back as she bused the latest empty table in the coffeehouse owned by her aunt Hilda. She quickly looked around, thinking that she might catch whoever it was.

The customers at the coffeehouse were mostly students from nearby John Adams College, where she went. Today the spring weather in Westbridge had also brought out a few retirees, who chatted or read or worked on crossword puzzles.

Sabrina blew out a tired breath. *You're imagining things,* she told herself. *You're just suffering from midterm burnout.*

The last few weeks had been hard. Balancing a col-

1

lege curriculum and a social life had turned out to be much tougher than she'd thought when she'd moved out of her aunts' house to begin school in the fall. *At least spring break is only another week away.*

Sabrina still hadn't decided what to do for spring break. But a lot of things could happen before then. A lot of things *had* to happen before spring break. Those things included writing papers as well as taking midterms. And then there was all that studying to do as well.

The little worrying sensation tingled at the base of Sabrina's brain again. The feeling of being watched grew. *Who is it?*

Then Sabrina spotted two college guys sitting at a table with open books before them. Both of them were looking at her. More than a little irritated, Sabrina walked over to them and said, "Okay, what are you looking at?"

The two guys swapped looks, then gazed back at her. "We've been trying to get your attention," one of them said.

"Well, you've got it now," Sabrina told him.

The guy pointed to the two empty cups on the table. "Uh, we really didn't want to bother you." He nodded toward the textbook Sabrina had left open at the end of the counter. "We're cramming for midterms, too."

Sabrina glanced at him. Okay, so he had the heavy-lidded, red-eyed gaze that most of the college students had at about this time. And if he hadn't slept in his clothes, he'd probably napped in them.

"Oh." Sabrina felt embarrassed. *Customers with empty cups will stare at you.* "What are you drinking?"

"Coffee."

Sabrina smiled. "Refills coming right up." She took the empty cups back to the counter.

Aunt Hilda was standing at the counter, doing paperwork when Sabrina got there. "So," Hilda said, "are the tips bigger when you harass the customers first to soften them up?"

"I thought they were staring at me," Sabrina said.

"They were," Hilda replied. "I could recognize the crazed I-want-a-refill look in their eyes from here."

"I think somebody's been watching me," Sabrina replied defensively.

Hilda put down her pencil, her attention now on Sabrina. "What are you talking about? Why haven't you mentioned this to Zelda or me?"

"Because I'm not sure," Sabrina answered. "Look, it's only been a couple of times. Until today."

Deeply concerned, Hilda scanned the coffeehouse. "Did you see the person today?"

"No. There's nobody there, Aunt Hilda." Sabrina sighed, wishing she hadn't mentioned anything to her aunt. "I haven't actually caught anyone watching me. That's why I haven't said anything before. It's just a feeling I've had a couple times."

Hilda looked at her. "Three times. Counting today."

Sabrina nodded. "But see? It's just like this." She waved out at the coffeehouse. "I get the feeling that

3

someone is watching me, but no one is there. I'm starting to feel like Chicken Little."

"Oh, but, honey," Hilda chided, "you can't take risks with something like this."

"I'm not taking risks. Both times it happened before, I made sure I walked home with a friend."

"You should have told Zelda and me."

"I was trying to take care of it myself. You know, be the responsible college person."

"A responsible college person tells her aunts," Hilda said. "And she alerts campus security."

"If I had anything more than a paranoid feeling," Sabrina assured her, "I would have. And I have told you. Three times is just too much. I'll be right back." She took the refills to the two college students and stopped on the way back for the plastic tub of dirty dishware she'd collected.

Hilda looked even more worried when Sabrina returned. "Maybe we should tell Zelda about this," Hilda suggested. "She could talk to the security department. Or maybe you can stay with us for a few days."

"Thanks, Aunt Hilda," Sabrina said, "but I'm not going to let this worry me that much." *Unless it gets worse.*

"It's one thing to be independent," Hilda said, "but don't let stubborn independence overrule common sense." She took the tub of dishes and started for the small kitchen in the back. "I thought you were distracted today because something had happened with the new guy."

Sabrina looked at her aunt. "New guy?" The new guy was something else she hadn't talked to her aunts about.

"You've had 'I've met a new guy' written all over your face for days now."

"Oh," Sabrina said, *"that* new guy." The sensation of being watched rattled across her shoulders again, raising goose bumps this time. She gazed through the coffeehouse windows.

Outside, bright sunshine poured down onto the streets. College students and neighborhood pedestrians passed in a constant parade.

Is someone watching me from outside? Sabrina walked over to the window, taking the small cleaning broom from behind the counter with her. *Like this is going to beat up a bad guy!*

No one on the street, though, seemed the least bit interested in her.

A small group came in, and for a while Sabrina was kept busy filling orders. Once the crowd was served, Hilda looked at Sabrina expectantly.

"What?" Sabrina asked.

"The new guy," Hilda prompted. "Give me the dish. I've been waiting for days. I promised myself I wouldn't pry."

"You did?" Sabrina thought that was highly unusual. Of her two aunts—and she loved them equally—Hilda had a tendency to pry more than Zelda did.

Hilda frowned. "No. Not really. Actually, I promised

Zelda I wouldn't pry." She paused. "That's not really working either, is it?"

"No, but that's okay. I haven't talked about him much because I don't know if he likes me."

Hilda took Sabrina's face in her hand and squeezed. "What's not to like?"

Sabrina took a deep breath. "His name is Cristoval Sanchez." Just saying his name out loud made her nervous.

"Cristoval," Hilda repeated. "Sounds intriguing. So where do you know him from?"

"Psych one-oh-one. Sits in the front of the class."

"That's good," Hilda said. "So I guess that means the two of you sit pretty close together."

"Opposite sides of the room. There are a lot of people in class. I'd seen him a few times before, but I'd never really noticed him."

"It's spring. Noticing others gets to be a priority around this time of year. What do you know about him?" Hilda returned her attention to her paperwork.

"He's tall and has dark hair so curly it hangs in ringlets. Dark skin. Brown eyes. He plays soccer and is very intense in class."

"And he's cute."

"Very cute."

Hilda sighed. "You know, there's nothing quite like romance in springtime. How long have you been interested in Cristoval?"

Sabrina looked around the coffeehouse. "Do you

think you could say it any louder? There may have been some people back against the wall who didn't hear your announcement."

"Sorry. I'm just excited for you."

"I don't think he even knows I'm alive."

"So how long has he not even known you were alive?"

"About a week and a half." Finished with the condiment tray, Sabrina slid it back under the counter.

"No mutual friends that might be able to give Cristoval a nudge?"

"Why does this whole *liking* thing have to be so complicated?"

Hilda looked at her. "It's been this way for years."

"Gotta get some low-fat creamers from the chiller," Sabrina said, changing the subject. At least she'd have a couple of minutes to herself without being watched or having Aunt Hilda busy "not prying." She walked into the chiller and went to the back. She bunched up her apron to make a pocket for the little plastic cups and started filling it up.

The cold clinging to the metal walls of the chiller suddenly seemed a lot more intense. In fact, it felt freezing inside the chiller.

Sabrina glanced at the walls and saw that the layer of frost clinging to them seemed to be growing by the second. *That's strange.* Still holding the apron full of low-fat creamers, she reached out to the wall.

Almost immediately, the frost leaped from the wall

and started tracking up Sabrina's finger. Then the chiller light exploded with a flash and went out.

This is too weird, Sabrina thought. Then the feeling that someone was watching her hit again. But how could anyone be watching her inside the dark chiller? She was alone.

Although the chiller was pitch-black, Sabrina easily made her way to the door. She bumped her hip against the hands-free release, but the door didn't open. She tried it again but quickly realized that she was locked in.

"Hey!" Sabrina yelled as she slapped the door. The feeling of being watched got stronger. "Who's out there? Who locked me in?"

A whispering voice came from the back of the chiller.

Sabrina turned. How had someone gotten in there with her? Her heart beat so fast she thought it was going to explode.

"Stay away. Stay away. Stay away," a dry, angry voice whispered.

"Who?" Sabrina gasped in disbelief. "Me?" The whispering continued, but she couldn't make out the words. Stay away from what? She pressed back against the chiller door.

Without warning, the door opened to reveal a tall figure framed by the light behind it.

Instinctively Sabrina zapped the tall figure, turning him into a toad. She stepped in front of the door so it couldn't close on her and lock her in again. She gazed down at the toad, which was staring back up at her intently.

"Sabrina!" Hilda cried from the doorway. "What do you think you're doing? You just turned Josh into a toad!"

Sabrina looked down at the toad on the kitchen tile. Josh was a prelaw student from Emerson College who also worked at the coffeehouse. He'd been Sabrina's first manager when she'd taken the job there, before Aunt Hilda had bought the coffeehouse. "That was Josh?"

"Rbbt," the toad said.

Chapter 2

Zelda Spellman stood in the center of the chiller after Hilda and Sabrina had closed the coffeehouse and Josh—returned to human form and not aware that he'd been a toad for a short time—had gone home. Zelda chanted a brief spell.

> *Though he or she has been hidden*
> *From every eye,*
> *Reveal to me now*
> *Sabrina's secret spy.*

Sabrina watched the magical sparkles shoot from her aunt's finger. The sparkles turned into a mushrooming cloud that quickly scoured the interior of the chiller. In a couple of moments the sparkles disappeared.

"Well?" Sabrina asked.

Zelda sighed disgustedly and placed her hands on

her hips. Blond and slender, she was wearing a black cocktail dress because she'd been attending a university function. When Hilda had bought the coffeehouse, Zelda had become a professor at John Adams College.

"I can't find anything," Zelda admitted. "If the spell worked, it would have revealed spy-eye prints."

"Spy-eye prints?" Sabrina asked.

"Sure," Zelda said. "Spy-eyes—whatever device your unknown watcher is using. Retina prints are probably even more individualistic than fingerprints. And a lot harder to copy, I might add."

"I didn't know that."

"That's because you've never gotten interested in witchcraft forensics."

"Witches have forensics studies?" Sabrina asked. She was amazed even though she knew she shouldn't have been. The Other Realm had plenty of secrets that she didn't know about.

"Of course they do," Zelda replied.

"At any rate," Hilda said, "you couldn't figure out who's been spying on Sabrina."

Zelda frowned but looked thoughtful. "No, and I don't like that at all. It means whoever is doing this is magical in nature and really good at it." She looked at Sabrina. "Sabrina, I know you like living in the house with your friends, but maybe Hilda's right. Maybe you should move back in with us for a few days. If you stayed home even for the weekend we might be able to find out what's going on."

"No," Sabrina said. "Look, I really appreciate the offer, guys, but my house is my castle. I'm not going to be scared out of it. Besides, if things get weird there, I can always zap myself back to your house."

Her aunts looked at each other for a moment.

"That is true," Hilda said.

"Of course it's true," Sabrina replied. "I'm a witch."

"Perhaps," Zelda said. "But you have to remember that whoever did this may not be mortal either. Anyone skilled enough in magic to do this might be able to do a lot more."

"But why?" Sabrina asked. "I haven't done anything to anyone."

Zelda walked over to Sabrina and smoothed her hair. "I don't know, sweetheart, but I promise you that we'll get to the bottom of this. I'll get a message to the Witches' Council when Hilda and I get home."

"In the meantime," Hilda added, "be careful."

Still worried about what had happened at the coffee-house, Sabrina zapped herself to the street corner near her university-owned house. She'd had to talk her aunts out of accompanying her.

She walked the half block to the house in the cool weather. Spring had warmed Westbridge, but it hadn't completely chased off winter. Her breath fogged in the night air.

Sabrina walked up the steps leading to her house. She'd never before noticed the shadows that crouched on either side of the steps, but she noticed them now.

She found herself holding her breath as she put her key in the lock and let herself in.

Even though she didn't have the creepy sensation of being watched, Sabrina quickly closed the door behind her. It shut with a bang that echoed through the large space that served as kitchen-dining-living area. The room was filled with people studying in groups. Pizza boxes and fast-food containers littered every surface that wasn't covered by books and notes.

"Hey, Sabrina," Roxie King greeted her from the dining table. She was dark-haired and pretty, dressed in casual jeans and a dark green pullover. She and Sabrina hadn't gotten along well when they'd first met and shared a room, but they were friends now. "How did your night go?"

"Oh, about the same as usual," Sabrina replied. "Got locked in the chiller. Nearly froze to death."

Roxie laughed and turned to the three other young women studying with her. "See? A sense of humor. What did I tell you?"

It was no surprise to see Roxie studying. She was attending John Adams College on an academic scholarship.

Miles Goodman occupied the floor, sitting cross-legged with a group of friends. Miles had unruly dark brown hair parted down the middle and a terrific smile. The orange rugby pullover, green shorts, and athletic socks he was wearing told Sabrina he'd probably come straight from soccer practice.

"There's still some popcorn," Roxie offered. "And

maybe some pizza hidden away in the back of the fridge. Morgan put it there."

Morgan was Morgan Cavanaugh, the twenty-one-year-old junior who supervised the university-owned house and lived upstairs. Morgan had a tendency to stash food or claim it as tribute for being supervisor.

"Hey, I'm not touching food Morgan has hidden," Sabrina joked. "She would know."

"Maybe she won't dust for prints this time," Roxie suggested. "Or maybe she hasn't counted how many pieces she hid."

"Morgan always counts," Miles said. "And she always dusts for prints. She doesn't buy into the 'But this is stuff I bought' defense even a little bit these days."

"She's not that bad," Sabrina replied.

"Yes, she is," Miles and Roxie said together. But their teasing was good-natured. Both of them liked Morgan a lot.

Sabrina decided that she was pretty lucky. Everyone in her house got along well. Not every house was like that.

"Well, it looks like you guys have everything under control," Sabrina said. "Studying anything I might be interested in?"

"American history since 1877," Miles said.

"Nope," Sabrina said. "That was last semester. We do have Psych one-oh-one together." She raised her eyebrows hopefully. "Any takers?"

Miles shook his head. "I'm gonna ace the psych test."

Sabrina glanced at Roxie.

"Anthropology," Roxie said.

"Not until next year," Sabrina replied. "And maybe not at all." Her lack of any real interest so far in anthropology might disappoint her mother—who was a professional anthropologist—but Sabrina knew she had to follow her own love of journalism.

Roxie nodded and looked sympathetic. "Sorry."

"It's okay," Sabrina said. "I'll just go to my room and do some independent studying." But independent studying wasn't nearly as much fun as cramming for tests college-style—all night, fueled by junk foods and arguments.

"Hey, before you go, I've got a message for you," Miles said.

"What?"

"I was at soccer practice earlier," Miles said, "when Cristoval Sanchez came up and started asking me about you. He found out we're housemates."

"Cristoval Sanchez asked about me?" Sabrina asked excitedly. *He did notice me!*

Chapter 3

"Yeah, Cris asked about you," Miles said. "You're kind of the only Sabrina Spellman I know. He takes Psych one-oh-one with us, you know."

"I know," Sabrina said. "But how did he know we lived in the same house?"

"You've brought my homework to me a couple times," Miles said. "He heard you talk to me about it."

"What did Cristoval want?" Sabrina's heart sped up a little as she waited for Miles's response.

Miles shrugged. "No biggie. Sounded more like a want-to-get-to-know-more-about-you thing than anything else. I just thought you might like to know."

"I do," Sabrina said. "Thanks, Miles."

"Oh, and he said he was going to see you in the morning."

"In the morning?" Sabrina thought frantically. The only thing she had planned for the morning was paint-

16

ing the house that was part of Professor Timmons's environmental science extra credit workshop. She didn't need the extra credit, but she was looking forward to painting the house for a family that needed the help.

Miles nodded. "At the house tomorrow. He's helping paint. Turns out that Professor Timmons the environmental science professor is dating Professor Sandhurst the speech professor. I guess they've kind of turned it into a joint project."

"All right," Sabrina said. "Thanks." She turned and walked to the room she shared with Roxie, her mind spinning with excitement. She hadn't given any thought to what she was going to wear the next morning to paint in, but now, with Cristoval going to be there, it suddenly seemed important.

Sabrina lay on her bed and stared out the window. She had the journalism book spread over her stomach, but she hadn't been able to concentrate on it.

Cristoval Sanchez asked Miles about me, Sabrina thought. She glanced at the clock by her bed and saw that it was after one o'clock in the morning. Roxie was still in the living room with her study group. Sabrina knew that in the morning, when she had to get up to be at the house for the extra-credit assignment, she'd regret not getting to sleep.

"Sabrina."

Startled, Sabrina jumped, recoiling from the sound of the voice before she recognized it as Hilda's.

Both of her aunts stood at the foot of her bed in their bathrobes.

"See?" Zelda said. "I told you we wouldn't wake her. Look at the shape she's in."

"You poor dear," Hilda cooed. She pointed up a glass of warm milk and brought it over.

Sabrina took the glass, taking comfort from the milk as well as the presence of her two aunts. "What are you two doing here?"

"We came to check on you," Hilda said.

"We couldn't sleep either," Zelda added. "We also did some checking around and found a spell that we think will help you. At least a little."

"What kind of spell?" Sabrina asked.

"A warding spell," Zelda answered. "Although we can't keep whoever your unknown watcher is from scrying on you in public, we can make your room scry-proof."

Scrying, Sabrina knew, was the magical ability of seeing other people and places through mirrors or a bowl of water. "Really?" The thought made her more excited than she would have thought.

"Yes," Hilda said. "I talked to Drell and got the Security Widget."

Drell was the leader of the Witches' Council. He was also one of Hilda's old boyfriends.

"Okay," Sabrina said excitedly, laying the journalism book aside. "So where is it, and what does it do?"

"It," Zelda said, "is right here." She opened her hand and revealed something purple and egg shaped. It looked suspiciously like one of the plastic eggs used at Easter to hide treats in.

"That's it?" Sabrina couldn't believe it.

"No, actually this is it." Zelda opened the egg shape to reveal a pink blob that looked like a cow's tongue coiled in on itself. It pulsated as if it was breathing.

Which meant that it probably *was* breathing.

"This is a Security Widget?" Sabrina asked doubtfully.

"Of course," Zelda said. "Touch it."

"I'd really rather not," Sabrina said, imagining the stomach-churning potential of such an experience.

"You have to," Hilda said, "to complete the spell."

"What spell?" Sabrina asked.

"Once the Security Widget is in place, no one will be able to scry into this room." Zelda shrugged. "Hilda and I aren't happy about the situation either. If no one can scry in, then we can't scry in to make sure you're all right."

Reluctantly Sabrina stretched out her hand and touched the Security Widget. The little creature felt as awful as it looked, complete with oily-slick skin.

But at Sabrina's touch the Security Widget bounded out of the egg shape and toward the wall behind Sabrina's bed.

"*Widgettttt,*" the creature shrilled. "*Widgetttt.*" In the next instant the Widget oozed into the wall and disappeared. However, a silvery sparkle showed under the wallpaper, across the ceiling and windows, and under the carpet.

"Now that the Security Widget is in place," Zelda said, "that should keep all those prying eyes out of your room. I'm sorry we can't do the whole house for you, but Security Widgets spread only so far."

"That's okay," Sabrina said. "Actually that's great because I was lying here wondering if I was going to get locked into my own room."

"Not now," Hilda said. "No one can see into your room now. You can at least get a good night's rest until we can figure out what's going on."

"I'm going to need it," Sabrina said, "because tomorrow morning is going to be a little different from what I thought it would be." She quickly told her aunts about Cristoval asking Miles about her.

"Don't worry, dear," Zelda said soothingly, patting Sabrina's hand. "It could just be that Cristoval is starting to notice you. After all, you have been trying to get his attention."

"I know. But now that I've got his attention, I'm a little nervous. I mean, what if he gets to know me and decides that he was better off not knowing me?"

"Sabrina," Zelda said, "everything is going to be just fine. You should just enjoy yourself. That's what I'd concentrate on."

Sabrina nodded. "I'll try." But she knew she was going to be nervous. She wanted to know what the morning would bring.

What the morning brought, Sabrina discovered bright and early, was a cat. At least, that's what it brought at first; then things got really interesting.

"Hey, wake up, sleepyhead. You're burning daylight

here. A guy can clean his whiskers and amuse himself with his tail for only so long."

Tail? Sabrina pushed the covers from her head and looked at the foot of her bed.

Salem Saberhagen, looking every bit like a black American shorthair cat, was curled up on the bed. He flopped his tail haphazardly back and forth.

"Salem?" Sabrina said.

"In the fur."

"What are you doing here?" Sabrina sat up. Despite all the tension of the night, she'd slept soundly and hadn't even woken. In fact, she felt almost rested.

Roxie, though, was asleep in her bed, papers and books scattered around her.

Not wanting Salem to wake her roommate and then go through the whole process of explaining a talking cat, Sabrina pointed up a pair of earmuffs on Roxie's head. *Have to remember to point those off,* Sabrina thought, *or she's going to freak when she wakes.*

"Hilda and Zelda were talking over breakfast this morning," Salem explained, "and I found out you were getting spied on."

"You came to check on me?" Sabrina smiled. "How sweet." Although Salem divided his time between her house and her aunts' house, sometimes she felt she didn't get to see Salem enough. Of course, there were also times that she felt she saw entirely too much of him.

Salem blinked his yellow moon eyes. "Sure. I came to check on you. And to let you know about the new business I'm starting up."

21

"Business?" Sabrina echoed. Alarms went off in her head. Salem didn't exactly operate on the straight and narrow, and he was always scheming.

"My card." The cat slid a business card out from under his furry body.

Sabrina took the card and immediately noticed all the small punctures.

"Tooth marks," Salem apologized. "Carrying the card from your aunts' house to here gave me a bad case of dry mouth. Maybe I could talk you out of a bowl of milk later." He coughed plaintively. "And some cereal in it while you're at it."

Sabrina read the card.

SALEM SABERHAGEN
Bodycat to the Stars
"I've got nine lives, and I'm willing
to risk them all to
help YOU!"

Sabrina saw that her aunts' phone number was listed. The hours given for taking calls happened to coincide with Zelda's and Hilda's regular times away from the Spellman home. She peered at Salem over the card. "Bodycat, huh?"

Salem preened, then straightened up. "How do you like my tough-guy look?" He slitted his eyes and laid his ears back, then raised one paw and flicked the claws out. When he hissed, he looked a little like Bela Lugosi playing Dracula, in Sabrina's opinion.

Sabrina struggled to keep from laughing. "Uh, that looks great. Really."

"Or maybe I should try to pull off a more genteel, dignified look." Salem turned to the side and peered over his own shoulder. He half-closed one eye but kept the other one open. "So what do you think? Maybe I should wear one of those pencil mustaches. Or, I know, a monocle."

"Salem," Sabrina said, "why do you need a look?"

"I want to have my picture on the card. Give my clients a face they can trust and believe in."

"What clients?"

"The clients for my bodycat business."

Sabrina sighed. *Maybe I'm just not awake yet.* "What are you going to be doing as a bodycat?"

"Why, protecting people, of course." Salem looked indignant.

Before being turned into a cat, Salem had been a warlock who had constantly been on the wrong side of the Witches' Council. The council had finally drawn the line when Salem had tried to take over the Mortal Realm. He'd been sentenced to one hundred years of penance as a cat, but even so, Sabrina wasn't sure if Salem would learn his lesson. He had a scheming and devious nature.

Sabrina glanced at the clock. It was almost seven. She was going to have to hurry to get to the house in time to start painting with Professor Timmons's morning crew. She turned her attention back to Salem. "Tell me again why I need the services of a bodycat?"

"I heard Hilda and Zelda talking about your mysterious watcher," Salem replied. "I kind of figured you'd need specialized help."

Specialized help, Sabrina thought, *is Aunt Hilda and Aunt Zelda.* Still, she didn't want to hurt Salem's feelings. He was pretty self-centered, but his heart was generally in the right place.

"What kind of specialized help are we talking about here?" Sabrina asked.

"I'll be there today to protect you."

Sabrina eyed the cat dubiously. As if he could read thoughts, he sat stiffly erect and puffed out his chest to make himself look bigger.

The effort caused Salem to start coughing and sneezing. He gazed up at Sabrina hopefully.

"Okay," Sabrina said, knowing she was probably going to regret her decision. "You can come, but I don't want you making a nuisance of yourself."

"Moi?" Salem asked, looking offended. "Why, I'm a professional. No one will even know I'm there if I don't want them to know." He straightened up theatrically. "I'll be a ghost, a shadow." He moved quietly, slinking across the bed as if stalking a mouse. "I'll be an unseen presence flitting through their ranks. A force for good. While they try to watch you, I'll be watching—*urk!*"

Salem toppled off the side of the bed.

"Watching *urk,* huh?" Sabrina asked. She kicked the covers off and got out of bed.

Only slightly embarrassed, Salem rose back up and put his forelegs on the edge of the bed. "I meant I'd be watching for the watcher."

It actually felt good to know that Salem was going to be watching over her like some kind of furry guardian angel. The thought that he had cared so much for her choked Sabrina up a little. There were a lot of good things about living on her own, but she'd walked away from a lot of good things as well. One of them had been a cat familiar who claimed to be willing to lay down his lives for her if necessary, just because he cared so much about—

"There is one more small item we need to discuss," Salem said, interrupting her warm and fuzzy thought.

"What's that?" Sabrina asked.

"My fee."

"Your fee?" Sabrina couldn't believe it.

"You expect me to risk one of my lives—maybe all of my lives—for nothing?" Salem gazed at her round-eyed.

"You're a beginning bodycat. I'm not paying a beginning bodycat to protect me."

"Okay," Salem said quickly. "Calm down. How about this? If you make it through the day without anything happening, then you pay me. That way you'll have gotten the work in advance."

"And you'll get paid for doing nothing if nothing happens."

"That's a pleasant prospect," Salem said, "but I prefer to think that just having me around may scare this vile perpetrator off."

"How is that going to happen if the vile perpetrator never sees you? 'Unseen presence flitting through their ranks' ring any bells?"

Salem was silent for a moment. "Just because I've printed cards doesn't mean I've worked out all the details. I'm a work in progress."

"Then you'll be paid when things progress," Sabrina said matter-of-factly. She glanced again at the clock on her dresser. "Uh-oh. Gotta go."

There was no way she wanted to be late for the painting assignment. The crew had only a short amount of time to get the house ready for the family they were helping. And then there was the whole prospect of Cristoval. Did he really want to talk to her? Was he really interested in her?

Chapter 4

Voices drew Sabrina's attention as she took her second break of the day. The painting at the house was going well, but she still hadn't seen Cristoval, although she had been looking for him. Another volunteer had said Cristoval was going to be late because he'd been up all night studying.

"Erica's doing this whole foresty thing in the kids' room," a guy in the tiny kitchen said excitedly when Sabrina arrived. "She painted little fluffy rabbits running through the forest on the wall."

"Catching all the field mice and bopping them on their heads?" Sabrina teased.

The student stared at Sabrina, awed at her suggestion. "No, but, dude, that would have so totally rocked. What she's got going on, see, is like this big bear hanging out in the forest. He's kind of like the friend to all the little forest animals."

Sabrina was intrigued. Erica Wilson had a real talent for art. Taking a bottle of cranapple juice and an energy bar from the snacks the professors had provided, Sabrina headed upstairs to the kids' room.

When she stepped inside, she was blown away by the fantastic job Erica had done, even after the description she'd just heard.

A sure hand had sketched a forest on the room's walls, but only some of the colors had been filled in so far. The forest was cluttered with leafy trees heavy with bright apples and oranges. Bushes heavy with blueberries and vines with thumb-size purple grapes ran amok. Birds of every color perched on tree branches and in the bushes. Besides rabbits, Erica had also drawn squirrels and mice.

A shaggy brown bear sat on a large stump in the center of the clearing. If the creature had been standing, it would have been over ten feet tall. The bear's nose was long and pointed and lent considerable character to his broad face. His huge front paws cupped a tiny nest of bluebirds. Inside the nest, the bluebird babies flapped their wings and had their mouths open as if they were singing.

"Erica," Sabrina said, "that is so incredible."

Sitting on the floor on crossed legs, Erica smiled and pulled her red hair from her face with the end of her paintbrush. Thin and tall, she wrapped her arms around her knees and flexed her shoulders. Paint stained her ripped jeans and ragged sweater, and drops showed on her bare toes. "Yeah, it's turning out really well, but it's going to take more time than I'd planned. I can finish up most of it today and get most of the rest of it blocked out, but it's going to take another two or three evenings to finish."

Sabrina walked around the room. "Has Professor Timmons seen it yet?"

"He was blown away. He agreed to give me extra time to finish this room. Spring break starts Friday afternoon. He said I can work that weekend and maybe a couple of days into spring break if I needed more time."

"I can't believe you'd give up your spring break to finish this wall."

"I love this wall," Erica declared. "I want those two little girls to feel safe and at home."

"They will," Sabrina assured her. "Any little girl would absolutely love this room."

Without warning, the feeling of being watched returned to Sabrina with full intensity. The cold chill spread across her shoulders.

Sabrina gazed around the room, trying to figure out where the feeling was coming from. She walked to the window and peered out. A few neighbors were outside working in their gardens or washing their cars, but no one seemed interested in the house.

But as she looked outside, Sabrina knew that the sensation wasn't coming from that direction. It was coming from inside the house. In fact, it was coming from behind her.

"What's wrong?" Erica asked.

"Nothing," Sabrina said, trying to cover her reaction. "Maybe I drank my water a little too fast. I just feel a little sick." That was no lie because her stomach was churning.

Erica got up quickly and padded barefoot toward the door. "I'll go get some paper towels. Just in case. I'll be right back."

Trembling with fear, Sabrina stared at the painting of the bear on the wall.

Somehow she wasn't at all surprised when the bear turned its head and glared at her. "I told you to stay away," the bear said hoarsely. "I warned you!"

Then the painted bear stepped out of the painting right at her. Before she could run, the bear was on her with a mighty pounce. It wrapped its forelegs around her and lifted her from the floor. For a moment Sabrina thought she was going to be treated to a WWF Smack-Down! takedown.

The bear shoved its muzzle into her face.

Ugh! Sabrina thought. *Bear breath!*

"Why didn't you stay away?" the bear demanded.

"Stay away from what?" Sabrina fought against the bear's grip but couldn't escape. "This house?"

"You're a foolish little girl," the bear said. "You're involving yourself in things you know nothing about."

Trying to buy time, Sabrina asked, "Then why don't you tell me what this is all about? That way, we'll both know."

"Don't play games with me!" the bear roared. It held Sabrina by the shoulders and shook her like a rag doll. The movement made its head thump against the ceiling.

Okay, Sabrina thought, *enough is enough.* She reached

out and pinched the bear's ear so hard that tears came to the animal's eyes. It reached for its ear with one paw and Sabrina squirmed free.

On her feet again, Sabrina immediately ran for the doorway. But the bear was fast and intercepted her before she could run through. It swiped at her with a large paw and knocked her sideways against one of the freshly painted walls.

Sabrina expected to smack up against the wall. Instead, she stumbled into the forest and tripped over an exposed, gnarled tree root. She touched the tree root she had tripped over, not believing it could actually be in the bedroom. Or maybe she wasn't in the bedroom anymore.

In the forest now, the bear rose to its full height in front of Sabrina. "Go away!" the bear ordered. "And stay away!" The bear threw its head back and growled again. Then the bear swiped at Sabrina again.

"Look out!" someone yelled.

Sabrina turned instinctively and caught a glimpse of someone running through the forest at her. In the next instant, they collided and Sabrina was spinning.

"Get out of here!" a male voice yelled. "Get out of here now!"

Sabrina ducked and threw herself to one side. She wrapped her arms around her head and zapped herself to her aunts' home.

Since it was Saturday and neither of them had anything really pressing planned, Hilda and Zelda were both at home. They were sitting at the kitchen table when Sabrina popped in.

Quickly, Sabrina filled in her aunts about the bear popping out of Erica's painting in the children's room.

"Are you sure this was a real bear?" Hilda asked when Sabrina had finished.

Sabrina had started pacing the floor as she talked. "It walked like a bear, it roared like a bear, and it had horrible bear breath. That's enough to convince me."

"But normally," Hilda said, "bears don't talk."

"You couldn't get this one to shut up." A frightening thought struck Sabrina. "Oh no! What if the bear is still running around the house?"

"Well," Zelda said, "we should check on that." She stood up from the table. "But we'd better be prepared just in case it is." She pointed at the three of them.

In the next instant, Sabrina found herself dressed in safari gear and carrying a big hoop net. She pushed her pith helmet back. "This doesn't look like a good idea."

"Oh, don't worry." Hilda waved her hand nonchalantly. "We've been bear hunting with Daniel Boone and Davy Crockett. There's nothing we don't know about bears. Except possibly why one would be in a house in—"

"Let's go," Zelda warned. She pointed all three of them away.

With her aunts at her side Sabrina stared at the painted wall, totally confused. Nothing looked out of place in the bedroom. The bear was even back on the wall, holding the small nest of baby bluebirds.

"I don't understand," Sabrina said. "When I left here, this room was the forest and that bear was moving. And someone else was in the room—or the forest—with me." There was no sign of her mysterious rescuer now.

Cautiously, Hilda approached the painted bear. She pressed her hand up against it. Nothing happened. "Well, it's not living now." She glanced over her shoulder. "Do you still feel as if you're being watched?"

Sabrina waited a moment, then shook her head. "No. The feeling is gone." The bear's eyes still followed her around the room, but that was an artistic trick and not part of whatever weirdness was following her around. She felt helpless.

At that moment footsteps sounded in the hall.

"That will probably be Erica—if she hasn't already come in here and found out I was missing."

"You might want to change back into painting clothes," Hilda suggested. "Zelda and I will go back home to try to figure out what to do next."

Sabrina nodded unhappily.

"We'll get to the bottom of this," Zelda promised, giving Sabrina's shoulder a reassuring squeeze. The aunts popped back to their house.

Sabrina zapped her clothes back to the painting outfit she'd had on earlier just before Erica entered the room with a fistful of paper napkins.

"Hey, are you okay?" Erica looked at Sabrina worriedly.

"I think so," Sabrina replied. "The sick feeling must just have been a temporary thing." She paused, uncertain how to ask the next question. "Did you happen to see anyone running from this room?"

Erica shook her head. "No, you're the only person that was in the room that I know of." She looked at Sabrina again. "Are you sure you're all right?"

Sabrina looked at the painted bear on the wall. "I'm fine." At least, she hoped she was fine.

"Hey, is everything all right in here?" a voice asked.

Turning, Sabrina spotted Cristoval Sanchez standing in the doorway. His dark brown hair formed cute ringlets, and although he was smiling, he looked a little worried. He stood there in stained jeans and a red sweatshirt with its sleeves hacked off.

"Everything's fine," Erica said. "Why wouldn't it be?"

"I don't know." Cristoval shrugged. "I thought I heard some weird noises in here, that's all." He glanced at the painted bear on the wall.

"No weird noises," Erica promised. Then she looked at Sabrina. "Unless there were weird noises while I was gone."

Sabrina shook her head but couldn't take her eyes off Cristoval. He was really cute, with warm hazel eyes that were green and then brown, and a nice smile, which was one of the first things Sabrina had noticed about him a week and a half earlier.

"I didn't hear anything," Sabrina said.

Cristoval looked embarrassed. "I guess maybe I've been studying for midterms too hard. I overslept this morning and didn't get here till late. And I had all those weird dreams last night." He had just the faintest accent when he talked, and it sounded totally awesome.

"What weird dreams?" Sabrina asked.

Cristoval shrugged. "You know: getting up late on test day, going to the wrong room, having to search frantically all over the campus for the right room, then sitting down at the test and not even being able to remember my own name."

Sabrina couldn't help but smile despite the tension and worry that had filled her. "I thought I was the only one who had dreams like that."

Cristoval grinned, which made him look even more adorable. "Not this week," he said. He shifted restlessly in the doorway. "You're Sabrina Spellman, aren't you?"

"Yes." Sabrina's heart thumped a little faster.

"I'm Cristoval Sanchez."

"Psych one-oh-one. I know. We kind of said hi to each other before."

Cristoval grinned again, and Sabrina liked the way his eyes flashed. "Yeah, we did, didn't we?"

An uncomfortable silence stretched out after that. Erica must have sensed something was going on. "Hey, if you'll excuse me," she said, "I've got a forest to finish painting."

Despite her recent scare, Sabrina couldn't help feeling interested in Cristoval. She wanted to get to know more about him.

"Hey, do you think we—" they both said at the same time.

Sabrina laughed, and it really felt good to laugh like

that after everything that had been going on. "I'm sorry."

"Me, too," Cristoval said, folding his arms across his chest and leaning against the door frame. "You go first."

"No, you. I didn't mean to interrupt."

"Guys," Erica said, sitting on crossed legs in front of the wall she was working on. "You're stumbling all over yourselves and having one of those I-think-I-forgot-how-to-do-this moments." She looked up at them with a straight face. She spoke in a deep voice. "I was just thinking maybe we could go get a coffee or a soda and talk a little." Then she made her voice high-pitched. "Oh, that sounds wonderful. I'd love to."

Sabrina laughed and Cristoval joined in.

"She makes it sound so easy," Cristoval said.

"There's a coffeehouse near John Adams," Sabrina said. "We could drop in there after we get done here."

"Cool," Cristoval said. "I'd like that very much."

"Hey, Cristoval!" someone shouted from downstairs.

Cristoval turned and shouted back down. "I'll be right there." Then he faced Sabrina again. "The guys. I guess they're kind of waiting for me. So we're on for the coffeehouse after we finish the work detail here?"

"Yes," Sabrina said. "I'd like that a lot."

Cristoval left the room, jogging back downstairs to the cheers and jeers of the people he was working with.

"Ooooh," Erica said after he'd gone.

Sabrina turned toward her. "Ooooooh?"

"Sparks," Erica said, dipping her brush in green paint to fill in more grass on the forest floor. "There was so much electricity in the air between you two that I thought my hair was going to stand on end."

Before she could help it, Sabrina felt a grin spread across her face.

"See?" Erica pointed her brush at Sabrina. "A goofy smile. A sure indication of chemistry."

Chemistry. Sabrina really liked the idea of chemistry, but she couldn't help looking at the painted bear on the wall and worrying more than a little. Cristoval had admitted that he'd gotten to the work site a little late. Had the creepy feeling of being watched not shown up until he had?

She sighed.

"What's wrong?" Erica asked. "Having one of those I-can't-believe-I-agreed-to-a-date attack of the jitters?"

"Maybe a little," Sabrina admitted.

"It'll pass. Cristoval is a really good guy." Erica switched brushes and went back to one of the bunnies she'd been working on, making the cottony tail a little fluffier.

"Do you know him?" Sabrina asked.

"I had two classes with him last semester: Universal Mythology one-oh-one and Legends in Archaeology. Legends was pretty cool. We discussed the possibility that earth was visited thousands of years ago by alien races and that Atlantis was really an alien outpost that got flamed in some kind of intergalactic war. Professor Thomsen makes a great case for it, but I don't really buy into aliens."

"Cristoval was interested in that?"

"Not the legends so much. But the concept of inter-dimensional traveling really got him."

"Interdimensional traveling?" Thanks to the linen closet in her aunts' house, Sabrina knew all about inter-dimensional traveling.

"Sure. The idea that sometimes people walking or driving down the street accidentally pop into other dimensions—alternate realities—that are really close to our own."

Sort of like visiting the Other Realm without using the linen closet, Sabrina thought. She stared at the bear painted on the wall. *Or like suddenly being thrown into a forest that can't possibly exist.* "So Cristoval really liked this interdimensional traveling idea?"

"He spent a lot of time talking to Professor Thomsen about it. They got into OBEs and that whole thing."

"Oooh-bees?" Sabrina repeated.

Erica dipped her brush into the paint again. "Out-of-body experiences. You know, where the conscious mind leaves the body for a little while. They say you can actually look down on your body."

"Okay, that's just too weird."

"Cristoval and Professor Thomsen got into talking about remote-viewing one day, and I thought that was pretty cool."

"More interdimensional-traveling stuff?"

"No." Erica leaned forward and added more texture to the forest grass. "The American and Russian military established programs years ago to spy on each other. They trained psychically gifted people as spies. Those people could sit in a room somewhere and spy on people half the world away."

"They watched people like that?" Actually, it sounded like scrying, which witches were able to do, but the scenario sounded way too disturbingly familiar to Sabrina. A little panic scratched at the base of her skull. *Okay. Calm down. This all sounds like stuff Aunt Zelda will be very familiar with.*

"Yes."

"And Cristoval was really into that kind of thing?"

"Not really," Erica said. "He was more interested in the mythology class."

"Mythology, huh?"

"Yeah. Cristoval really got into it. His family is from Mexico, and a lot of the coursework concentrated on Central American myths. He's a bright guy, Sabrina, but he's a little shy. At least, that's what I've seen of him."

"Thanks for filling me in," Sabrina said. "Guess I'd better get back to my work crew before they wonder if *I* accidentally walked into some other dimension."

"They probably have walls that need painting there, too," Erica joked.

"Terrific. More work." Sabrina headed for the doorway. "You're doing a really good job on that wall."

"I'm trying," Erica said. "I want those kids to feel as though they've stepped into another world when they walk into this room."

"I can believe it," Sabrina said. "I know they will, too." She walked outside and heard teasing voices coming from below. Looking over the banister, she saw that

Cristoval's work crew was giving him a hard time about being late that morning as well as returning late to work.

Cristoval took all the teasing good-naturedly. Then, as if feeling Sabrina's eyes on him, he glanced up. For a moment worry darkened his face. When he saw her, though, his face lit up in a smile.

Immediately, a zing fluttered in Sabrina's stomach. It wasn't exactly the kind of zing she felt with Harvey Kinkle, but it was a zing all the same and it felt pretty good.

It would have felt even better without the bear episode this morning, Sabrina realized.

Cristoval's friends grabbed him and pulled him back toward work. He glanced up and smiled at Sabrina again, shrugging a what-can-you-do? look at her.

Sabrina sighed, wondering what she was going to do. She also wondered about Salem. He was nowhere to be found. *Some bodycat!*

Chapter 5

"I was born in a small village south of Puerto Vallarta," Cristoval said later that evening. He and Sabrina had taken a back booth in the coffeehouse after they'd finished the painting detail. "My mother's family is from there, and my grandfather still lives there with my grandmother. My grandfather is a fisherman. He's got a small boat, and he goes out every day to bring in the catch. Grandmother helps him prepare the fish, then my grandfather pedals his bicycle down into Puerto Vallarta to sell them to the restaurants."

Sabrina saw the love Cristoval had for his grandparents. "Sounds picturesque but also like a lot of hard work."

"It *is* a lot of hard work," Cristoval agreed. "Until I enrolled at John Adams College, I went out on my grandfather's boat almost every day." He ran his fingers through his curly ringlets. "I'd been going out on the boat with Grandfather since I was three or four. My mother used to totally freak. But nobody is safer on a boat than my grandfather. He taught me how to sail and how to fish."

"Sounds wonderful."

"It is. Have you ever been to Puerto Vallarta?"

"No," Sabrina answered.

"Are you familiar with Mexico?"

"My mother is an archaeologist. I went on some digs with her when I was younger. But I haven't seen her for a while."

"Is your father an archaeologist, too?"

"No. He's an . . . ambassador." That was true enough, Sabrina thought. Her father was a political mediator in the Other Realm. Until she'd gone to live with him for a time she hadn't known how busy he really was.

"Now, that's an important job. See? You're much more interesting than I am."

Sabrina laughed. It was surprisingly easy to be relaxed with Cristoval. "So your grandmother and grandfather run the family fishing business. I guess your mom helps them?"

Sadness filled Cristoval's eyes. "Actually, my mom passed away a few years ago."

"I'm sorry," Sabrina said.

Cristoval nodded. "Please don't feel embarrassed or uncomfortable. You couldn't know without asking, and unless we ask things we're not really going to get to know each other, are we?"

"No."

Cristoval smiled. "My father, Gabriel Sanchez, is captain on a cruise ship out of Puerto Vallarta. The ship is called the *Pacific Sunset*."

"Now, that's a cool job," Sabrina said. "It must be really tough going on cruises nearly all year round."

"It's not as exciting as it sounds. Since I was sixteen I've worked on my father's ship part of every summer. There's a lot of work involved in making sure the passengers have a good time. The only time I ever see Dad really rest is when he's on vacation."

"And I'll bet he doesn't go on cruises."

"No way," Cristoval agreed. "He goes sport fishing, which is how he met my mom. My dad was fishing the waters near where my grandfather fishes a lot. My dad ran into my grandfather's boat and ended up having to pull it back to shore before it sank. Dad wasn't a captain then so he didn't have very much money. My grandfather told my dad not to worry about the damage, that he could fix the boat in a couple days. Anyway, my dad couldn't just leave the boat for my grandfather to fix, so he stayed to help."

"And that's how he met your mother?"

Cristoval nodded and looked into his empty cup.

"What did you do on your father's ship?" Sabrina asked.

"I was a dishwasher and sometimes an entertainer."

"What kind of entertainer?"

A small crimson blush stained Cristoval's features. "I play guitar, piano, and the drums, so I filled in a few times with the band. I also danced in some of the musical numbers. One summer *Grease* was the big production event. I was understudy to the lead. The guy got sick during the cruise, and I got to perform two days in a row."

"That must have been exciting."

Cristoval shook his head. "It was one of the scariest things I've ever done." He paused. "But I do wish my mom had gotten to see me play that role. She had passed away by that time, but she and Dad were already divorced."

"My parents are divorced, too," Sabrina said. "It's kind of hard to deal with sometimes."

"I know. My grandfather told me that my mom and dad were just too different. My mom still held to a lot of old beliefs, a lot of the old traditions from the Toltec people. My grandfather is like that, too, but he's a lot quieter about it. My dad is a totally modern guy."

"You'd have to be to be a cruise ship captain," Sabrina said.

A sheepish grin lit Cristoval's face. "So, have you heard enough about me yet?"

"You haven't scared me off," Sabrina said. She found herself liking him just a little more. It was one thing to be with a guy who listened, but it was really special when the guy actually talked about real stuff as well. She liked the way the coffeehouse lights flickered in his eyes.

"You're going to be a business major?" Sabrina asked. She and Cristoval were walking back toward her house.

44

Cristoval nodded. "My dad told me if I was going to get a college degree, business would be a good area to go into." He shrugged. "It made sense to me, so I started taking courses in it."

The night was dark and overcast, which lent a chill to the wind, but Sabrina didn't notice it. Her hair blew around her shoulders, and her cheeks burned a little from the cold.

"What are you majoring in?" Cristoval asked.

"Journalism."

"Thinking of becoming a reporter?"

"Maybe. I don't know yet, but I do know I like writing a lot." Sabrina watched a car go by. While she was walking next to Cristoval in the cold night it seemed hard to remember all the weird stuff that had been going on for the last week and a half. Being with Cristoval made everything seem normal somehow. "When I was talking to Erica earlier she said that she'd taken a mythology class with you."

"Yeah. My mom used to tell me the stories about this magical land called Xhalchiat. It was supposed to be this old mystical kingdom of the Toltec people who were gifted with special powers." Cristoval shrugged and grinned self-consciously. "Her stories were filled with all this grand adventure, heroes and villains, monsters and treasures—everything a boy could hope for."

"Your mom must have cared a lot about you."

"I'm sure that she did." Cristoval was silent for a moment. "My grandfather didn't really care for my mother telling me all those old stories. Grandfather always told her that the past needed to stay in the past. And this from the guy who still pedals to the market to sell his fish."

Sabrina returned Cristoval's amused smile. *That smile,* she decided, *is becoming habit-forming.*

"Mom just started telling me the stories whenever my grandfather wasn't around. Doing that kind of made the stories more special because the time belonged to Mom and me."

"That's why you took the mythology courses."

"My grandfather would never tell me any of those old stories," Cristoval said. "He wouldn't let my grandmother tell me those stories either. When I visited my father, I went to libraries to find books to read during the cruises. I read a lot of mythology, but I didn't find anything that mentioned Xhalchiat. Who knows? Maybe my mom made it up."

Sabrina listened quietly, enjoying the sound of Cristoval's voice. He was one of the nicest guys she had met in months. And then there was the whole zing thing happening in her stomach.

"Did you ever ask Miles about Xhalchiat?" Sabrina asked.

"No. I know he took the class with me, but you're the first person I've ever told about my mom's stories." Cristoval looked at her and shook his head. "I really don't know why I did except that you are so easy to talk to."

"I know. I feel the same way about you."

Cristoval looked up the block and said, "You know, I could have sworn it was farther to your house."

Sabrina saw her house and felt a little disappointed. She wished the evening could last longer.

"Hey," Cristoval said when they reached Sabrina's door. "I just want you to know I had a really good time tonight."

"Thank you," Sabrina said. "I had a really good time, too."

"If it's okay with you, I'd like to do this again."

Are you kidding? It would be great *with me!* But out loud Sabrina just said, "Sure. I'd really like that."

Cristoval smiled. "When do you think you could stand to see me again?"

Before Sabrina could answer, the feeling of being spied on returned. At first she thought the feeling might be from Roxie or Miles checking out the window to see who was standing at the door. But there was no way either of them could make her feel like that.

In the next instant, a light flashed—like a bulb burning out—and Cristoval grayed over like a scene from an old black-and-white movie. He stood frozen for a moment and then disappeared entirely.

Chapter 6

Not believing what had just happened, Sabrina stepped forward and reached into the space where Cristoval had been standing. Only empty air greeted her touch.

"Cristoval!" she called. The feeling of being watched didn't go away. She turned and scanned the neighborhood, trying to figure out where the watcher was watching from. And what had made Cristoval vanish?

The door opened, and a rectangle of light from inside spilled out onto the porch, bathing Sabrina in its glow. Roxie stood in the doorway, looking curiously at Sabrina.

"Did you decide to take up standing alone outside in the dark?" Roxie asked.

"Oh," Sabrina said. "I was just gazing at the constellations and boning up on astronomy."

Roxie looked up at the overcast sky. "There's not a star in sight, let alone a whole constellation."

And there's no Cristoval in sight anywhere, either.

48

Sabrina peered through the darkness anxiously. *He can't have just disappeared!*

But there was no other explanation.

"I'm imagining the constellations that are usually there," Sabrina explained. *Okay, that's so not one of my best.*

Roxie glanced back at Sabrina. "And I know your schedule. You're not taking astronomy."

"But I might be someday. Besides, I get tired of Miles beating me at *Who Wants to Be a Millionaire* all the time."

"Miles beats everyone when it comes to astronomy questions. He always will. Get used to it." Roxie stared at Sabrina. "Where have you been? Not still painting?"

"I went out to dinner with a friend." *Who has since vanished off the face of the earth!* Sabrina thought about that for a moment. Once the police found out Sabrina had been the last person seen with Cristoval, who was now missing, how long would it be until she was arrested? And if she did answer questions about Cristoval's disappearance and told people that he had disappeared in front of her eyes, how long would she stay out of a mental institution?

"Are you coming in?" Roxie asked.

"In a minute," Sabrina answered.

"Suit yourself, but it seems a little chilly out here to me." Roxie stepped back inside the house and closed the door.

I've got to call Aunt Hilda and Aunt Zelda, Sabrina

thought. *They'll know what to do—maybe.* She sincerely hoped they would.

"Are you trying to keep me in suspense, or what?"

Recognizing Cristoval's voice, Sabrina spun around and found him standing where he'd disappeared. He acted as though nothing had happened.

"Where did you go?" Sabrina asked.

"Are you joking? I've been standing right here waiting for your answer."

Staring at Cristoval, Sabrina suddenly understood that he had no recollection of disappearing. "What do you know about interdimensional portals?" she asked.

Cristoval shrugged. "Only what I learned in class."

"You don't travel to other dimensions?" At least, Sabrina thought, that would be one possible solution to how he disappeared.

"No." Cristoval smiled uncertainly. "This is some kind of joke, right?"

He doesn't know! Sabrina realized. "Right. A joke." She forced a laugh to show him how funny she thought it was.

"How about going out again tomorrow?" Cristoval asked.

Sabrina hesitated, realizing that the prying eyes that had been on her had also disappeared. Was there a connection?

"We can bring our psych books and make it a study date," Cristoval offered.

The front door to the house opened again. "Hey, Sabrina, while you're out here stargazing, I want to know if I can borrow—" Roxie stopped speaking when she noticed Cristoval. "Oh, I'm sorry. I thought you were alone."

"Whatever it is, just take it," Sabrina replied.

Roxie hung around for a moment more, then said, "If you're sure it's okay." She closed the door again.

"Roommate," Sabrina explained. "We kind of look out for each other. In a noninvasive way. At least, most of the time."

"I see."

"Tomorrow night sounds great," Sabrina said.

Cristoval smiled. "I shall be looking forward to tomorrow, Sabrina Spellman."

"Cristoval sounds like a very nice young man," Zelda said.

"Except for the flicker-disappearance thing," Sabrina agreed. She was sitting with her aunts at their kitchen table later that night.

"Well, I haven't met a guy yet that hasn't had a few faults," Hilda commented. "Maybe Cristoval disappeared on you, but he did come right back."

Zelda frowned at her sister. "I don't think that is quite the issue we're discussing. Cristoval apparently isn't aware of his disappearance."

"I don't know what I'm supposed to do," Sabrina said.

"Well, honey, maybe you're not supposed to do anything right now," Zelda replied.

"That doesn't mean you should stop seeing him, though," Hilda said.

Zelda shot her sister a look.

"Well, it doesn't."

"And what if Sabrina disappears with Cristoval one day? Have you thought about that?"

Hilda was silent for a moment. "Okay, I'll admit I hadn't thought about that."

Zelda pointed at the table and set up two fresh mugs of tea for Hilda and herself. A cup of hot chocolate with a generous dollop of whipped cream appeared in front of Sabrina.

"We're three experienced witches," Zelda said, "one of whom has her Ph.D. Surely among us we can come up with some kind of answer. How long has Cristoval been disappearing?"

Sabrina looked back at both her aunts. "Well, don't ask me. He's never disappeared in psych before."

"We don't exactly have an abundance of information about Cristoval," Hilda pointed out. She looked at Sabrina again. "Are you sure he's not a warlock?"

"He doesn't have *warlock* stamped on his forehead," Sabrina answered. "And you know how you get that feeling sometimes when you come across someone from the Other Realm that they're, well, from the Other Realm?"

Both aunts nodded.

"Well, I don't get that from Cristoval. He seems like just a guy. A really great guy, but just a guy."

"A guy who disappears spontaneously and then reappears is *not* just a guy," Zelda said.

"Miles would say it was an alien abduction," Sabrina

said, sipping her hot chocolate. "You know, where aliens beam you up into their ship and do all kinds of weird experiments on you."

"We're familiar with that," Zelda said.

Sabrina's jaw fell. "You are?" She never ceased to be amazed by how much she didn't know about her aunts.

"We've been abducted more than once," Hilda added. "But the second time was part of a Club Mars package vacation."

"I guess it's possible," Zelda said thoughtfully. "Alien abduction also accounts for the 'lost time' victims suffer, when they're unconscious on the alien ship."

"That's why you always feel so rested after a Club Mars vacation," Hilda added.

Zelda looked at her niece. "Do you think Cristoval is the victim of alien abduction, Sabrina?"

Sabrina shook her head. "I don't know what to think."

"Well, get more information about Cristoval when you see him again," Zelda suggested. "Maybe we'll get one clue that makes sense."

"I'm going to see him again tomorrow night," Sabrina replied.

"During midterms?" Hilda asked. "I've got students falling asleep all over the coffeehouse trying to catch up for midterms. I know your grades are good, but—"

"Cristoval is a four-point-oh student," Sabrina said. "Neither one of us is really worried about midterms."

"But you want to be prepared for them," Zelda insisted.

"Exactly," Sabrina agreed. "Which is why we're having a study date tomorrow night."

"Good for you."

"A four-point-oh student?" Hilda repeated. "Brains *and* good looks?"

"I know," Sabrina admitted worriedly. "It's too good to be true, isn't it?"

"You can have the bathroom first tonight," Roxie offered. She lay stretched out on the bed in the room she and Sabrina shared, scribbling notes furiously into a spiral-bound notebook.

"Thanks. I'm really beat."

"Well, I'm not surprised. Midterms, volunteering, and—oh, yeah—dinner with a gorgeous guy." Roxie sounded envious.

"I didn't exactly plan this," Sabrina explained. She took a fresh towel and her toiletry bag from her dresser drawer.

"I don't see you postponing it till spring break either." Roxie sighed deeply. "Sorry. I don't mean to be such a grouch. And if I had to, I'd study straight through to exams rather than take a rain check on someone like Cristoval."

Sabrina glanced across the room and made sure the curtains were pulled shut. She assumed that the Security Widget was still in place and doing its job. Or maybe whoever it was wasn't spying on her, but spying on Cristoval. But who would spy on Cristoval? And why?

* * *

Okay, enough with trying to figure out answers for questions that you don't totally know yet. Sabrina had enjoyed a nice hot bath, complete with scented bath oil, but had racked her brain constantly until she had a headache.

Dressed in her pajamas, she brushed her teeth. All she wanted to do was go to bed and get whatever sleep she could. Her back and arms ached from all the painting, and even though the evening had been exciting, it had also been exhausting spending it with Cristoval.

Suddenly, a gurgling noise erupted from the sink.

Mouth still flecked with toothpaste foam, Sabrina stepped back.

Water bubbled up from the sink as if from a drinking fountain, spraying straight up. The stream grew until it formed a round shape as big as a softball. Then an old man's withered face pushed out one side of the water stream. Cold eyes fixed on Sabrina.

"You were told to stay away, girl," the creepy-looking man said.

Startled, Sabrina asked, "What do you want?"

"You're meddling with things that don't concern you, witch." The stranger's face had a hooked nose and deeply set eyes. Thin hair was pulled back tightly in a ponytail that reached the creature's shoulders.

"I don't even know you," Sabrina protested. "Tell me what you think I'm meddling in, and I'll—I'll—"

"Stop?" the man asked.

"Well, I'll at least think about it." Sabrina was angry.

She had been nervous for a week and a half, and she had no idea who or what this guy was, or what she was supposed to do.

The man growled suddenly, and his water head started to spin like something in a horror movie. Then the growl changed into an ululating scream.

The softball-size head broke free of the water and hurtled straight at Sabrina.

Chapter 7

Sabrina whipped the towel from her shoulder and raised it in front of her. She caught the water head in the towel, wrapped it tightly, and felt it burst. Water that wasn't soaked up by the towel rained down onto the tile floor.

Sabrina eyed the sink suspiciously for a moment before lowering her drenched towel. She jumped when someone pounded on the bathroom door.

"Hey, are you all right in there?" Roxie asked worriedly.

"I'm fine."

"It didn't sound like you were fine. What happened in there?"

Sabrina looked at the water on the floor. "I just spilled some water on the floor. It's no big deal. I'm going to clean it up." *And I'm also going to get to the bottom of this,* she promised herself as she bent down to clean up the mess.

As the week progressed and students finished their midterms, John Adams College slowly turned into a ghost town. Every day as she walked home from her latest exams, Sabrina saw more cars and taxis lined up in front of the dorms. Students were wasting no time in evacuating for spring break.

Posters advertising spring break parties flapped in the breeze. A lot of people had been excited about the parties on campus until it got time to stay or go. Most went.

Now, on Thursday, Sabrina wished she was one of them. Miles and Roxie had plans to leave on Monday, so they still had the weekend together after Friday's exams. Still, Sabrina was majorly bummed.

She had seen Cristoval every night that week. It was just so easy to spend time with him even when most of what they did involved preparing for midterms.

On Wednesday, though, Cristoval had told her he had already made plans to fly down to Puerto Vallarta to help out his father with the spring break cruise.

Captain Sanchez wanted his son aboard to help with the college students. Sabrina knew Cristoval would go. If there was one thing she had learned about Cristoval, it was that he took his responsibilities seriously.

Sabrina walked across a nearly empty parking lot and tried to be happy. She and Cristoval had agreed to go to a spring break party at the student union, so at least they'd have tonight. She hoisted her book bag over her shoulder a little higher, trying in vain to find a more comfortable position. Today, for some reason, the book bag felt as though it weighed a ton.

At least there hadn't been any more encounters of the spying kind. Whoever the hawk-nosed man was, he had evidently decided to give it a rest. *Or maybe he pulled something in his neck when he did the bathroom scene.* Cristoval hadn't pulled a vanishing act since the first date, and Sabrina was beginning to think maybe she had imagined that entirely.

"Hey, Sabrina! Wait up!"

Sabrina turned around, recognizing Cristoval's voice instantly. Her heart sped up, and she knew she probably had a grin on her face. At the coffeehouse, Aunt Hilda didn't miss a single opportunity to tease her about the goofy smiles Sabrina wore lately.

Cristoval jogged up to her, carrying a basket in one hand. Today he was wearing khaki pants and a blue oxford shirt left unbuttoned over a bright red shirt featuring a screened print of a Toltec temple. *Puerto Vallarta* was printed above the temple, and *Pacific Sunset,* the name of Captain Sanchez's ship, was printed below.

Seeing the shirt on Cristoval, Sabrina felt as if her heart was going to break. Suddenly, a week sounded like such a long time.

"Hey," Sabrina said, forcing herself to be bright and cheery. *I'm going to be unhappy while he's gone, but there's no reason he should feel guilty.*

Cristoval had also explained that while he was aboard ship he would have phone privileges. It would be no problem for him to call Westbridge two or three times a day and talk long into the night.

"I've been looking everywhere for you," Cristoval said. "I got through with my exam early and thought I'd make it over to your building before you finished yours."

"Sorry. I finished my exam early, too. I guess I was more prepared for environmental science than I thought I was."

"Well, you did have some help preparing for it." Cristoval smiled.

One of the things I'm really going to miss, Sabrina thought, *is that smile.* "Yes, I did. And thank you very much."

Cristoval shook the basket in his hand. "Your line is supposed to be something like, 'What's in the basket?' "

"Who are you supposed to be? Little Red Riding-Hood?"

Cristoval shook his head. "Not even close. Gee, and I'd come to expect such bright flashes of perception from you, Señorita Spellman."

"I think my brain is burned out from all the study sessions and exams this week." *Not to mention thinking about you.*

"Good. Then I've come just in time to rescue a damsel in distress."

That line is so hokey, Sabrina thought, *but Cristoval makes it sound so natural.* Still, she wasn't going to let him off easy.

"Rescue?" Sabrina raised her eyebrows.

Cristoval presented the basket he held in one hand. A

red- and white-checked cloth covered the contents. He pulled the cloth from the basket with a flourish, like a magician performing a well-rehearsed act.

Inside the basket were sandwiches, chips and dip, cheese and crackers, strawberries, and a foil-wrapped bottle of sparkling grape juice.

"That's a feast!" Sabrina exclaimed.

Cristoval shrugged. "After I walked you to your place last night, I went down to the store and picked up a few things. I know I didn't ask, but I was hoping that maybe we can have lunch."

Sabrina took him by the arm. During the last few days, that had gotten easy and natural. "I think it's very . . ." She stopped with the word *romantic* on her lips. *That's all I need to do: throw the R-word out there.* "Thoughtful." She nodded. "I think making a picnic lunch is *very* thoughtful. So where are we eating?"

"Let's go to the park," Cristoval suggested. "It's a warm day. If that's okay."

"It's great," Sabrina said, feeling more cheery.

"I've been thinking," Cristoval said quietly.

Sabrina struggled not to choke on the chicken salad sandwich she was eating. "Thinking about what?"

They were seated side by side at a picnic table under a broad oak tree near the center of the park. Sabrina had helped Cristoval spread the picnic lunch out on the red- and white-checked cloth. He'd even brought a single long-stemmed red rose and a small vase to put it in. They drank the grape juice from disposable plastic champagne glasses that Cristoval admitted he thought were corny but he really wanted corny for this lunch. Nearby, a group of small children played with their toys and on the jungle gym.

"Thinking about you," Cristoval said. "I've been doing that a lot these past few days."

"I guess your friends are getting tired of my name." Sabrina laughed. Josh, Roxie, and Morgan were all getting tired of her talking about Cristoval.

He smiled at her. "I don't think I have as many friends as you do."

"There are a lot of people who know you," Sabrina objected. "You're a major soccer player at college. Miles told me that."

Cristoval shrugged. "I guess so, but I just don't open up to people as easily as you seem to."

"You couldn't prove that by me, Cristoval Sanchez. From my perspective, you're very social and very open."

"That's what I'm talking about, Sabrina." Cristoval gave her a serious look. "Coming here to Adams wasn't easy. And it hasn't been easy really getting to know people. I've never told anyone everything that I've told you."

Sabrina felt flattered and didn't know what to say. "I'm having a good time, Cristoval. For the first time in a long time, I'm not as worried about things as I have been."

Cristoval breathed out deeply. "Well, maybe being worry free during spring break would be a good idea."

"Worry free?"

"It's just that I had this idea."

"Ideas are good," Sabrina prompted.

Cristoval only half-smiled at her. "This one may be a little sudden."

Sabrina gestured to the remains of the picnic lunch. Judging from what was left, they had both been starving. "Ideas always seem to go better on a full stomach."

Reaching into the bottom of the picnic basket, Cristoval took out a card. "I got this for you, but I don't want to freak you out."

"Don't worry. It takes a lot to freak me out. And I love cards. Actually, I have a card waiting for you at my room. Sort of a going-away/remember-me-while-you're-gone card. And that just goes to show you that Hallmark makes a card for almost every occasion."

Cristoval laughed. "Mine isn't Hallmark. I didn't think they had a card for what I wanted, so I just drew my own." Looking nervous, he handed her a card, with an envelope inside it.

Sabrina removed the envelope. The drawing inside the card was done in crayon, but she could tell that Cristoval had spent considerable time on it.

The drawing showed a luxury cruise ship at sea. A cerulean sky hung over the ship, and palm trees stood tall on the island the ship was sailing for. The people aboard ship were shown playing games like volleyball and shuffleboard, and there were even kids swimming in a big swimming pool.

Across the bottom was a single question: "Hey, Sabrina, want to come to Puerto Vallarta with me?"

"The tickets are in the envelope," Cristoval said. "I've got you booked on the same flight to Puerto Vallarta that I'm on. If you think you can stand the company." He gave her a halfhearted smile. "If you've got something else planned, I'll understand. This is kind of last-minute notice, but I hadn't counted on meeting someone like you, Sabrina."

Sabrina shook her head, not believing what Cristoval had done. "I can't accept this. It's too much. If I had known I was going to meet you, I'd have saved up money from my job at the coffeehouse."

"Look, it's not as much as you think. My dad gets a lot of freebies from the airlines and the cruise ship owners because of his job. The air tickets didn't cost much at all by the time my dad's comp privileges kicked in." Cristoval pushed out his breath. "Please say yes. I'm already feeling like I've made the biggest blunder in my life by assuming you'd rather go with me to Puerto Vallarta than do whatever else you'd planned for spring break."

"There's nothing I'd rather do," Sabrina said. "But I can't just take this and—"

"It won't be just fun in the sun," Cristoval apologized. "In order to get my dad to pull rank to get the tickets at the last minute, I had to guarantee him that you'd be willing to work on the cruise ship at least part-time while you were down there."

"A job?"

Cristoval acted really nervous. "It was the only way I could swing it. If I hadn't already promised my dad that I would be there for him, I'd stay here at school with you and picnic every day in the park, go to movies, or anything else we could find to do."

"No," Sabrina said. "Having a job waiting makes it easier to go."

It took Cristoval a moment to realize what she'd said. "Go?"

Sabrina nodded, feeling thrilled and happy. Spring break wasn't going to be such a bummer after all.

"You'll go?" Cristoval asked excitedly.

"Yes," Sabrina said. "I'll go." *Although I don't know exactly how I'm going to break it to Aunt Hilda and Aunt Zelda.*

"Hey, Sabrina, that's great!" Cristoval grabbed Sabrina in his arms, hugged her tight, and then released her. "Sorry! Sorry, I really didn't mean to get that carried away. I just never—"

Before Cristoval could say another word, he grayed over and flickered, and then disappeared.

Chapter 8

Again the feeling of being watched washed over Sabrina, as sticky and cold as near-frozen honey. One of the little boys playing nearby stood staring at Sabrina and the place where Cristoval had been.

Sabrina looked around frantically. Since that first night in front of her house, Cristoval hadn't disappeared again. He had also never brought up the disappearance.

So far, neither Aunt Hilda's nor Aunt Zelda's investigation into Cristoval's past had turned up any indications of magical involvement. Aunt Hilda had even gone so far as to check with Drell and the Witches' Council regarding the Alien Abduction Grievance Committee. Cristoval hadn't been on any of their lists either.

The little boy approached Sabrina curiously and looked up at her. "How did your fwiend do dat?" the boy asked.

Sabrina tried not to be worried. The last time Cristoval had disappeared, he had reappeared no worse for the experience. Sabrina had no reason to believe the same thing wouldn't happen again.

"I don't know," Sabrina told the little boy honestly. "I hope I can find out."

Cristoval reappeared before she could say any more. He was still talking. "—just never thought that you'd want to go, and I'm really excited about the idea." This time, however, his face was pale.

The little boy screamed and laughed as he ran off. "Mommy! Mommy! Come watch what this man can do! He can do magic!"

Sabrina studied Cristoval. "Are you sure you're all right?"

Cristoval looked a little defensive. "Of course I'm all right. Why wouldn't I be all right?"

"For a minute there," Sabrina said cautiously, "you looked like you were somewhere else."

Cristoval shook his head. "It's nothing to worry about. I think I'm just tired. I've had too much going on lately." He looked down at her and smiled. "Of course, a lot that has been going on has been really good."

"So what were you thinking about?" Sabrina asked.

Embarrassment turned Cristoval's face red. "I guess I blanked out on you, huh?"

Sabrina held her hand up with her forefinger and thumb only a fraction of an inch apart. "Maybe a little."

Cristoval turned his attention to the picnic table and began cleaning up. "I don't know. I guess I usually think about those stories my mom always told me.

She's been on my mind a lot lately. I wish she could have met you."

"Me, too," Sabrina said. She lent Cristoval a hand, and they soon had the table cleaned off.

"I'm sorry," Cristoval said. "But I have to go help the afternoon janitors get the shift done at school. If we don't get finished in time, I'll never make the pre-spring break dance tonight."

"That's okay," Sabrina replied. "I've got a shift at the coffeehouse anyway. Then I have to pack for the trip to Puerto Vallarta."

"If we move fast," Cristoval said, "I should have time to walk you to your place before I have to go to work."

"I'd like that." Sabrina slipped her arm through Cristoval's, and they started walking. Going to Puerto Vallarta with Cristoval sounded like a lot of fun, but she had to wonder when he was going to disappear next. She couldn't help feeling that he was in danger of some kind.

"Going to Puerto Vallarta with Cristoval isn't a good idea right now, Sabrina. We're not going to allow it." Zelda Spellman placed her hands on her hips.

Sabrina knew when her aunt did that she really had her mind set. Sabrina glanced at Hilda, who was sitting with them at the Spellman kitchen table.

Hilda held up her hands. "No. I totally agree with Zelda on this one, Sabrina."

Sabrina was bummed. The usual strategy in the Spellman household was to divide her aunts. Hilda had a softer side and normally could be counted on for support. *Things aren't exactly normal, though, are they?*

"Think of my trip to Puerto Vallarta as an experiment," Sabrina suggested, smiling brightly.

Zelda crossed her arms and leaned back from the table. She raised one eyebrow suspiciously. "An experiment?"

"Sure. You know, with controls and catalysts." Sabrina thought furiously. With Aunt Hilda siding with Aunt Zelda, the only way she'd get to go was to get Aunt Zelda to agree.

"Controls and catalysts," Zelda repeated.

"We know I'm being watched here," Sabrina said, "but if I go to Puerto Vallarta and no one spies on me, we'll know that whoever is spying on me is local."

"And what if you're spied on in Puerto Vallarta?" Hilda asked.

Sabrina opened her mouth—then closed it. *I didn't think of that.*

"That's why we're aunts," Zelda said.

"Besides that," Hilda said, "if Cristoval isn't mixed up in this, he's got real problems of his own."

"Maybe I can help him," Sabrina suggested.

"How?"

"I'm a witch," Sabrina said. "I like Cristoval a lot—"

Hilda patted her hand. "Honey, we know you do."

"And I want to help him," Sabrina said.

"How are you going to do that?" Zelda asked.

"By watching him," Sabrina said. "If he keeps disappearing, maybe I can find out why, report back to you, and we can fix it. I'll be flying down to Puerto Vallarta like a mortal, but I'm a witch and I can pop myself back here in the blink of an eye."

"If you haven't disappeared along with Cristoval," Hilda reminded.

"I can't just sit here and do nothing," Sabrina complained. "Cristoval disappears. I'm being watched. Bears are stepping out of paintings. Watery heads are popping out of faucets. Who knows how bad this is going to get before it gets better?"

Neither aunt spoke.

Feeling a little more optimistic, Sabrina continued. "If whoever is watching me is local, at least I'll get a break down in Puerto Vallarta."

"Taking a break from your problems isn't going to solve them," Zelda said.

"Staying here hasn't exactly solved them either," Sabrina pointed out.

Hilda looked a little more worried as she turned to her sister. "Sabrina is right, you know."

Zelda started to argue, then sighed. "I know."

Sabrina brightened. "Then it's settled? I can go?" She got excited again.

"Maybe I'd feel better about your going if Cristoval wasn't disappearing the way he is," Zelda said.

"Okay," Sabrina said, "I admit it: Cristoval has a problem. One, I might add, that he apparently isn't even aware of. I can't do anything about my own problem now, but maybe I can help him with his. You've always told me that when I couldn't work on my own problems I should help someone else with theirs. I want to help Cristoval."

"And your tan," Hilda said.

"Maybe a little," Sabrina said.

"We could keep an eye on them, you know," Hilda said.

Sabrina was mortified. "Spy on me? Ugh, no thanks. I've had enough of that to last me a lifetime. I like my privacy, and I don't want even you invading it. Sorry."

Zelda looked thoughtful. "You know, with Sabrina in Puerto Vallarta maybe it would be easier to find whoever has been spying on her. We might have a better chance of tracking the spell over a long distance."

"That sounds good," Hilda said.

Sabrina got more excited. She was practically airborne.

"Of course," Zelda mused, tapping a thoughtful forefinger against her chin, "distance isn't going to be a factor in tracing Sabrina's spy if the spell is coming from the Other Realm."

"It's got to make some difference," Hilda said. "At least Sabrina can have a little fun. After midterms and this, she could probably use it."

Oh, I can use it, Sabrina thought. *Lots and lots of it.*

"What if she disappears?" Zelda asked.

"Oh, she's not going to disappear," Hilda replied confidently. She pointed at Sabrina's arm.

Instantly, Sabrina felt an awkward weight on her wrist. She looked down and saw an ugly purple and yellow bangle bracelet. "Ugh," she said, and tried to take it off. The bracelet wouldn't budge. "Hey. This is stuck."

"Yes," Hilda replied, "and you're stuck with it."

"What is it?"

"A Throckmorton's tracking device?" Zelda said, surprised.

"Exactly," Hilda said. "A Throckmorton's tracking device. Guaranteed to give off signals no matter what realm you're in."

"Signals?" Sabrina asked.

Hilda patted her hand. "Yes. While you're wearing a Throckmorton's tracking device, Zelda and I will be able to find you anywhere. We don't have to worry about you disappearing. If you do, we can find you."

Sabrina looked at the ugly bracelet. Being traceable sounded more secure but not very much fun. And the colors were just . . . just . . . *ewwww!* "Okay, guys, not wanting to sound unappreciative here, but does this thing come in any other colors?"

"No," Hilda said. "And if you decide to take it off, or if it somehow *falls* off, you'll be popped back to this house immediately." She pointed at the kitchen ceiling. Immediately, a siren and a flashing light appeared there. "You'll also set off the alarms."

Sabrina looked at the huge siren. There was no way anyone could sleep through that. She sighed in defeat.

"It's the only way I can feel good about you going to Puerto Vallarta, Sabrina," Zelda said.

"Me, too," Hilda said.

"Okay," Sabrina agreed. At least she'd be getting to

go to Puerto Vallarta with Cristoval, and maybe she'd get to the bottom of at least one of the mysteries facing her.

By early Friday afternoon, Sabrina and Cristoval were seated side by side on the jet. He didn't say anything about the bracelet she wore. As they talked excitedly, the hours flew by. Then exhaustion caught up with them.

"I'm sorry," Cristoval said. "I can barely keep my eyes open."

"That's okay," Sabrina said. "Why don't you take a nap and I'll read a magazine or something." They had stayed later than they had planned at the pre-spring break party at the student union the night before.

Cristoval was asleep in seconds.

Sabrina watched him for a moment, then gazed around the darkened airplane. The majority of the passengers had grown quiet, immersed in books or listening to headsets. The familiar pinging of handheld game devices let Sabrina know that some of the kids were still awake.

A flight attendant passed by and handed out extra pillows and light blankets for passengers who wanted them. Sabrina took a blanket and placed it over Cristoval. He was sleeping so deeply that he didn't even move.

Sabrina snuggled back in her seat and closed her eyes. Before she drew her next breath, the distinct feeling of being watched returned.

Her eyes snapped open, and she gazed around the plane. No one seemed overly interested in them. *But with magic involved, whoever is watching doesn't have to be on the plane.* She thought of the old hawk-faced man immediately. She recalled the spell Aunt Zelda had recently taught her from her *Discovery of Magic* handbook. She picked up the half-empty glass of water she had left from her last snack. She thought the water would be clear enough for her spell.

Sabrina had used scrying spells before, but she had never tried to scry on someone scrying on her. She whispered the spell under her breath so no one would hear.

> *I spy*
> *With my little eye*
> *The one who watches me,*
> *And I do it on the sly.*

Sabrina pointed at the glass of water. Immediately, a picture began to form in the liquid. She spotted the old hawk-faced man sitting on a huge stone throne in a large room. The man wore a red garment that looked like a kilt and a towering feathered hat, and in one hand he held a long, feathered spear. A heavy, ornate necklace made of interlocking stones fixed to beaten metal lay against his thin chest. He wore wristbands in the same stone-and-metal design.

Now I see you, Sabrina thought excitedly.

The old man chanted and peered at a ceramic bowl on the stone table in front of him. The bowl was painted with geometric designs in red, white, black, yellow, and green. He raised a hand and dropped bright blue powder into the ceramic bowl.

Immediately, the powder caught fire in the water. Tall pale green flames leaped up from the bowl. The old man nodded his head in approval and leaned back in the stone throne.

What are you up to? Sabrina felt her breath lock in the back of her throat as she anxiously continued watching. Then she felt the pull of the blanket she had placed over Cristoval. Distracted, she turned to look at him to see if he had rolled over in his sleep.

Instead, Cristoval flickered, on the verge of disappearing again.

Without thinking, Sabrina grabbed Cristoval's hand before it could vanish. Something pulled on him, yanking him into wherever it was he disappeared to. For a moment Sabrina thought she could hold him, but in the next instant the force sucked her into it with Cristoval.

When she opened her eyes again, Sabrina was no longer on the plane. She gazed in wide-eyed wonder at the jungle around her. Branches of huge trees blotted out the sun overhead, but she knew it was day wherever she was from the way light filtered down through the trees.

She was standing on the grassy bank of a slow-moving river. The gurgle of the current echoed through the trees, and in the distance monkeys howled and birds screeched.

A twitching motion above her drew Sabrina's attention. Swishing back and forth was the tail of a jaguar lounging on a tree limb only a few feet above her head.

The jaguar was beautiful, its glossy yellow coat spotted by black markings. Long and lean, the big cat appeared to be more interested in sleeping than in her. It yawned, black lips pulling back to reveal large fangs. Then its pink tongue lolled out, almost giving the jaguar a comical look.

At least, it looked comical until Sabrina remembered that jaguars were carnivores. She'd probably be a quick snack for the jaguar. She started backing away, trying not to make any sudden moves that might catch the attention of the big cat.

Sabrina felt her wrist for the Throckmorton's tracking bracelet. All she had to do was try to remove the yellow-and-purple band and immediately she'd be transported back to her aunts' house. Her fingers closed over the hard plastic.

"Sabrina, what are you doing here?"

Surprised, Sabrina wheeled around to find Cristoval standing nearer the river by a dugout canoe and smiling at her. *Cristoval?* She released the bracelet, knowing she couldn't leave him there by himself.

Cristoval was now wearing a blue breechcloth and leather sandals, and was shirtless. A hunting knife hung at his hip, and a gold necklace and thick wristbands completed his ensemble.

"I guess I came with you," Sabrina said. "We were on the plane together. Remember?"

She hoped her aunts didn't choose that moment to check on her through the Throckmorton's bracelet. She felt certain she could take care of Cristoval as well as herself.

Cristoval took a deep breath. "Yeah. We're still on the plane. This is just one of the dreams I have about the place my mother told me about. Pretty cool, huh?"

"Uh, yeah," Sabrina agreed. "Pretty cool." *Except that we're really* not *on the plane. And I don't know how we're supposed to get back.* "What is this place?"

"This is Xhalchiat." Cristoval dragged the dugout canoe into the river. "These dreams I'm having lately are really weird." He held the boat for Sabrina. "Climb in. I'll hold the boat."

"Maybe we should just go back to the plane," Sabrina suggested.

"We're already on the plane." Cristoval smiled at her as if she'd told him a joke. "This is just a dream. But I like these dreams. They're usually a lot of fun." He frowned a little. "Except for this latest batch of dreams, that is."

If I get wet here, Sabrina wondered, *am I going to be wet when we return to the plane? I mean,* if *we return to the plane.* She pointed to Cristoval and herself, then tried to point them back to the plane. When that didn't work, she tried to point them to her aunts' house, but that didn't work either. *We're trapped here!* The realization was frightening. There were few places a witch could be trapped.

None of them were fun.

Deciding she had nothing to lose and not wanting to offend Cristoval, Sabrina clambered into the canoe. "So what's different about these new dreams?"

"Every time I dream about Xhalchiat lately, I'm on this river." Cristoval pulled himself into the dugout canoe. "I know where I'm supposed to go, but it seems to be taking forever to get there."

"Where are you supposed to go?" Sabrina asked. Her attention was drawn to a flock of brightly colored parrots flying across the river in front of them. A group of monkeys swung through the branches on either riverbank. *Okay, so we're leading a circus.*

"To the end of the river." Cristoval took a paddle from the bottom of the canoe and started pulling it through the water.

"What's at the end of the river?"

"Wherever it is I'm going," Cristoval explained patiently.

This is so *not working for me,* Sabrina thought unhappily. "Don't you think it's a little odd that your dreams of this place have changed?"

Cristoval shrugged and kept paddling. "I don't know. My mom told me stories about this place, so I've been thinking of it for a long time. These dreams are the first ones that I've had that haven't been about Xhalchiat the way it was in my mom's descriptions."

"What was Xhalchiat like then?" Sabrina asked.

Cristoval watched the scampering monkeys and laughed at their antics. "It was a great place to be. Everything here was magical. The animals could talk, there were adventures to go on, and all the people got along. They all depended on one another, you see. They farmed and they built the great city of Xhalchiat with their own hands."

"They're all waiting at the city?"

"I don't know."

"Don't you think it would be better if you knew what was waiting?"

Cristoval smiled. "Sabrina, this is a *dream*. Part of the fun of having a dream is waiting to see what happens next. Haven't you ever noticed that when you know what is going to happen next you're generally in a nightmare?"

In a way, Sabrina thought, *that makes sense.* But she also knew that she wasn't dreaming and that she had a really bad feeling about what was coming up.

Sabrina stared down the river, noticing that it gradually got wider and the water ran faster. Sporadic sunlight dappled the river surface, turning the brown water emerald in places.

Suddenly, a massive head rose from the river directly in front of the canoe.

Instinctively, Sabrina grabbed the sides of the canoe and held on. She thought the creature looked like a hippopotamus, but it was too big to be one.

"Has this ever happened in your dreams before?" Sabrina asked as the hippo thing wiggled its ears and swam at them. Its head was at least three times as large as the dugout canoe.

"No," Cristoval answered calmly. "As I said, a lot of

things about the dreams have been changing. You've certainly never been here before." If the thought that he was about to be eaten by a monster twice the size of a Greyhound bus had entered his mind, he didn't show it.

In the next instant, the monster's jaws gaped wide and swallowed the canoe, Cristoval, and Sabrina.

Chapter 9

When Sabrina opened her eyes, she was back on the plane. Her pants were still soaking wet from boarding the canoe. Cristoval, however, was perfectly dry and still asleep.

At least there wasn't a monster in sight.

Sabrina pointed her clothes dry and concentrated on trying to get her heart to slow down. Maybe the dream *hadn't* been real, but it had felt real enough. And now she was wide awake and worrying.

She briefly considered popping herself back to Westbridge to talk to her aunts. But what was she going to tell them? She didn't know what had happened. And she was willing to bet that Cristoval would only believe he'd had a dream and would freak if he found out Sabrina had really been in it with him.

Glancing at the half-empty glass of water on the tray before her, Sabrina peered into the melted ice. The old, hawk-faced man had disappeared. Again she tried the scrying spell her aunt Zelda had taught her, but her finger only fizzled. She didn't know if the man had somehow sensed her and blocked her spells, or if she couldn't find him because he wasn't watching Cristoval or her.

Since Cristoval and the other man had been similarly dressed, Sabrina felt pretty safe in assuming the man was more interested in Cristoval than in her. But if the man was watching Cristoval, why had he started watching her?

She was still missing some piece of the puzzle, but she wasn't sure what it was. She thought briefly about telling her aunts what had happened, then decided against it. Hilda and Zelda would make her come back home. And if they did that, there might not be any way she could help Cristoval. Until she knew things were beyond her control, she wanted to stay to help him.

Beside her, Cristoval stirred and woke. He blinked at her sleepily and smiled. "Sorry. I know I'm not much company right now."

"That's okay," Sabrina said. "I'm so tired I'll probably be asleep any minute now." She hesitated, wondering how to broach her next question, then decided to be direct. "So, while you were sleeping did you have any dreams?"

Cristoval smothered a yawn with one hand and nodded. "Yeah. And it was a doozy. In fact, you were in it with me. We got eaten by some kind of river monster."

"I'll take a rain check on that if you don't mind."

"The entertainment on the *Pacific Sunset* will be a lot better," Cristoval promised.

"And maybe not so final." Sabrina looked into his hazel eyes. "You said you dream a lot about the place and the stories your mother told you."

"Yeah."

"And lately your dreams about the place have been changing," Sabrina said, knowing full well that the only time Cristoval had told her that had been in the dream just moments ago.

"I didn't know I told you that." Cristoval looked surprised. "Man, I must really tell you everything."

"Do you remember when your dreams started changing?"

Cristoval nodded. "Yes, that's easy. I had the first one of these new dreams of traveling down the river, just before or just after we started noticing each other in psych."

Okay, if you take a look at the coincidence factor— which I'm really willing to do at this point—that's got to mean something, Sabrina thought. *But what?*

"I'm very pleased to meet you, Señorita Spellman," Captain Sanchez greeted Sabrina.

As she shook his hand, Sabrina decided he was an older version of Cristoval. Lean and compact, he was dressed in captain's whites and stood ramrod straight, his captain's cap folded smartly under his left arm as he took her hand briefly in his right and bowed. Captain Sanchez was bald with a short-cropped fringe of hair around his head but wore a neat goatee. "I hope you enjoy your time aboard the *Pacific Sunset* while you are in Puerto Vallarta."

"I'm sure that I will," Sabrina replied. "After everything Cristoval has told me about the ship I don't see how I couldn't."

Captain Sanchez helped them with their suitcases as they made their way through the airport.

"You'll be staying aboard the ship tonight, if that is acceptable, Señorita Spellman," Captain Sanchez said as they went past the line of small shops and restaurants on the main level. "Otherwise, I'm sure I could get you a room on the mainland."

"Staying on the ship will be fine."

Captain Sanchez nodded. "I assure you, even the crew's quarters aboard ship are quite well-equipped."

"No," Sabrina said. "I'm good." She really didn't want any special attention, and she figured Cristoval would choose to stay on board to spend more time with his dad. Sabrina wanted to stay close to him in case any more weirdness happened.

Outside the terminal, Captain Sanchez led them to a line of waiting taxis. He helped Cristoval stow the luggage in the trunk of the first taxi in the line. Captain Sanchez took the seat in front with the driver in the compact taxi, leaving the backseat for Cristoval and Sabrina.

Father and son chatted amicably with each other in Spanish. Sabrina was tempted to point herself up an instant understanding of the language, but she decided their privacy was more important. Plus, a good knowledge of Spanish was something Cristoval would have expected her to mention before now.

Sabrina watched the city flow by as the taxi whipped through the streets toward Marina Vallarta, where the luxury cruise ships moored when they were in port. Night had fallen only a couple of hours earlier, and the city was lit up in a festive manner.

The taxi pulled up at the marina in less than fifteen minutes. Sabrina gazed out at the moonlit Bahía de Banderas, which Cristoval told her translated as the "Bay of Flags." Awed by the sight of the tall-masted fishing boats lining piers set away from the cruise ships, she was at a loss for words. Even at night the port was lively and busy, filled with boisterous voices. Recorded Mexican music intermingled with American rock blasted into the streets from speakers inside and outside the restaurants and businesses, and Sabrina felt the mixed rhythms vibrating inside her.

A golf cart stood awaiting their arrival. Captain Sanchez transferred the luggage to the cart, then offered to take Sabrina and Cristoval to dinner at a nearby restaurant.

Cristoval hesitated, glancing at Sabrina.

"Unless you would rather go by yourselves," the captain said. "I would totally understand."

"Well, I wouldn't," Sabrina said. "Cristoval told me he hasn't seen you since Christmas vacation. If anything, I should check in at the ship and let you two have some time to yourselves." *Please tell me you think that's a bad idea.*

"No, Sabrina," Cristoval said. "We'd love to have you."

Captain Sanchez cocked his head and nodded. "My son speaks truly, Señorita Spellman. A man could not enjoy a good meal without the company of a charming woman, and I mean to treat you to a good meal because I know the chef personally. It just would not be the same."

"Now I see where Cristoval gets his charm," Sabrina said, smiling and feeling flattered.

"Tell me, señorita, how is my son these days?"

Sabrina sat across from Cristoval's father at a round table at the little restaurant to which Captain Sanchez had taken them. Although the restaurant wasn't as big or as flashy as many of the other restaurants in the marina area, the meal had been fantastic. A band trio played live music on a small stage strung with red jalapeño pepper lights.

Cristoval had gone over to another table to say hello to a group of crew members and entertainers from the *Pacific Sunset*.

"He's good," Sabrina said. "He did well on his midterms, and he's a good student. He seems really okay." *If we don't count those disappearing adventures of his and popping into a strange world.* "I've actually known him for only a short time."

"He told me that." Captain Sanchez studied her, and the look he gave her made her feel uncomfortable.

Sabrina brushed at her hair self-consciously. "Is something wrong?" *Do I have a piece of lettuce stuck in my teeth and don't know it?* She covered her mouth with one hand just in case and checked with her tongue. She didn't feel anything.

"Pardon my behavior, Señorita Spellman," Captain Sanchez apologized.

"Please call me Sabrina, Captain Sanchez."

"As you wish." Captain Sanchez watched Cristoval intently.

"Maybe I should be asking *you* how Cristoval is," Sabrina said.

"You see him for yourself." Captain Sanchez smiled slightly. "He's healthy and bright and friendly. He is a very good person to have at your side on a cruise. I've seen Cristoval walk into situations where tempers were flaring. Yet he seems to know instinctively what to say to the people involved to get them to reconsider their actions. I used to call him the little peacekeeper. Of course, he was much younger then."

"He's a good guy," Sabrina said.

"He's always been very steady and very dependable." Captain Sanchez turned his attention back to Sabrina. "You have been the only surprise my son has brought me in years."

"Me? Why?"

Captain Sanchez allowed the server to refill his coffee cup and waited till she left to resume speaking. "Please don't think me rude."

"I don't think I ever could," Sabrina promised before he could go on.

"Cristoval has been around a lot of girls," Captain Sanchez stated. "In the fishing village where he lived with his mother and grandparents, onboard the *Pacific Sunset* when he worked summers with me, and, of course, at college in Massachusetts." He paused. "But never once has he ever asked to bring a girl with him from college or from that fishing village."

Sabrina nodded, wondering where the captain's speculations were going.

"Then Cristoval calls me this week out of the blue," Captain Sanchez went on, "and asks me to make arrangements to have you flown out here."

"I hope that wasn't too much of an imposition," Sabrina said.

Captain Sanchez waved the thought away. "No trouble at all. My only point is that Cristoval has always been such a thinker. He hardly ever does anything without planning."

Remembering the picnic lunch on Thursday and the way that Cristoval had set up the dating schedule for them without making her feel left out of things, Sabrina had to agree.

"I only know, señorita," Captain Sanchez said, "that there must be something very magical about you to have awakened such impulsiveness in my son."

Magical? Sabrina forced herself to stay calm. She hadn't even pointed up anything since she'd gotten off the plane. She watched the captain as he watched his son.

"There's something else on your mind," Sabrina said after a moment. Cristoval continued laughing and talking with his friends from the ship's crew.

"Perhaps," Captain Sanchez readily agreed. "You are an intuitive young lady."

"I think that even an unintuitive one could have guessed that one," Sabrina said. "What is it?"

"Has Cristoval talked to you about his mother?"

"Yes."

"She was a very special woman. Despite our divorce, we remained close in ways. She was always very superstitious, though, and it was one of the causes of our discontent with each other. She had her head full of old myths and legends, and I didn't want Cristoval too deeply involved with those things."

"What myths and legends?" Sabrina asked.

Captain Sanchez shook his head. "It doesn't matter. However, I find myself being somewhat superstitious these days in spite of myself. Cristoval's mother always insisted that he would have to be carefully watched once he turned nineteen."

"Is Cristoval nineteen?" *How could I have forgotten to ask about something like his birthday?* Sabrina couldn't believe it, but somehow the subject hadn't ever come up.

"*Sí,*" Captain Sanchez responded. "He turned nineteen less than three weeks ago."

The time frame suddenly clicked into Sabrina's head. "Three Wednesdays ago?"

Captain Sanchez pulled out a worn black schedule from his pocket and flipped through it. "Yes. His birthday was three Wednesdays ago."

Sabrina watched Cristoval. *Was it just coincidence that Cristoval and I noticed each other on his birth-*

day? And then there was the matter of his dreams changing concerning the mythological land that his mother had told him about. Maybe, if Sabrina hadn't ended up in one of those dreams, she might have dismissed the occurrence as a subconscious thing on Cristoval's part. His mom had told him something would happen when he was nineteen, and his dreams of that place had changed as a result. They'd learned about that in psych class.

"What I'd like to ask," Captain Sanchez said quietly, "is that you keep an eye on Cristoval for me. I think he will spend most of his free time with you, on the ship and off. And I think that if both of us are looking after him then things will be much better."

"I will," Sabrina replied.

Captain Sanchez shook his head. "Maybe we'll both discover that I'm merely being an overly protective father and am worrying for no reason. Then we can have a good laugh later."

If you knew everything I know, you'd be even more worried, Sabrina thought. She felt really bad that she wasn't telling him all she knew. But there was no way to do it without revealing that she was a witch.

She watched Cristoval and tried to make herself believe that everything was going to be all right.

"How's it going?"

Sabrina took the glass of lemonade Cristoval handed her and said, "Thank you."

They were standing in the *Pacific Sunset's* stern area

the next day, Saturday, and even with the three-hour time difference, the morning had come early. The bay spread out around the luxury cruiser as it sailed through the sparkling green water. Gulls flew across the blue sky, mixing with brightly colored parasails. While the birds flew freely, the parasails were towed at the ends of steel cables from small boats below. Waves rolled in and made the much smaller craft rise and fall, but the *Pacific Sunset* hardly budged. Strolling the deck was almost like walking on solid ground.

Sabrina sipped the lemonade and sighed in delight. "Everything is going fine. Although being a lifeguard at the pool can be a real pain."

Cristoval grinned. He looked tanned and healthy in ship's whites. "I told you this wouldn't be easy."

"I believed you."

"Still, I hope you manage to have some fun."

"It's good," Sabrina said. "Really. It was fun leading aerobics for the morning athletes and being shuffleboard referee. I didn't know there were so many ways to cheat."

Cristoval laughed. "If you give people enough free time, most of them will find ways to be creative with it."

"The lifeguard detail really threw me, though. I'd forgotten how energetic kids can be. If I had to blow my whistle one more time my ears were going to explode."

"I could maybe put you in a dance routine later," Cristoval suggested.

"No, thank you," Sabrina said. "I'm going to be hosting the checkers championship this afternoon."

"Good. We should be back at Puerto Vallarta by six this evening."

At the moment the *Pacific Sunset* was on a shakedown cruise after having work done on the engines. Captain Sanchez had briefed the crew and passengers that morning. Late Sunday morning they'd head south toward Manzanillo, stopping at a few ports along the way.

"If you're up to it," Cristoval said, "I'd like to show you around the boardwalk of the marina. If you're in Puerto Vallarta, you've got to see El Faro."

"Great," Sabrina replied. "What's El Faro?"

Another white-uniformed cruise attendant called Cristoval's name and spoke to him rapidly in Spanish.

"I'll show you later," Cristoval promised. "Gotta go."

Sabrina sipped her lemonade as she watched him go. They hadn't seen each other very much since that morning, but the evening was sounding promising.

Unless Cristoval performed one of his disappearing acts. All last night and all day, Captain Sanchez's words had run through her head.

Maybe I haven't been able to keep much of a close eye on him today, Sabrina thought, *but tonight should be no problem.*

El Faro turned out to be the official marina lighthouse. The structure stood 110 feet tall and was a working lighthouse for the harbor. El Faro also featured a circular lounge that catered to the late-night crowd.

Cristoval escorted Sabrina there only a short time before sunset. They sipped drinks, listened to the live band, and watched the sun slowly sink into the Pacific. For long moments Puerto Vallarta stood steeped in the final red and gold of the sun's rays, then the night invaded with bruised purple that gradually turned indigo.

A few minutes later, Cristoval took Sabrina by the hand and led her out into the night. He guided her down the boardwalk, which he had told her was called the Marina Malecón.

"What did you think?" Cristoval asked.

"The sunset was beautiful," Sabrina said. "Why did we leave so soon?"

Cristoval stopped. "I'm sorry. We could have stayed."

"No, that's okay. I was just wondering. There seemed to be a party in El Faro."

"There *was* a party in El Faro," Cristoval confirmed. "After being onboard a crowded cruise liner today, I thought maybe staying in the lighthouse would be a little too much. But I did want you to see the sunset."

"I'm glad," Sabrina said.

"But now," Cristoval said, smiling, "we're out to see the town. There are a lot of things to see. And I can tell you about them. I did some of the walking tours along Marina Malecón a few summers, you know."

"No, I didn't know," Sabrina said.

Cristoval smiled again. "Well, now you do."

Sabrina got lost in all the information Cristoval recounted of the city's history as well as the background of the local businesses. The air rolled in from the sea, salty and a little chilly, but it smelled and felt wonderful.

She wore a simple black dress, and Cristoval had traded his ship's whites for charcoal gray slacks, a dark blue shirt, and a black blazer. It was the most dressed up either of them had been since they'd been together, but that made the occasion more special. Sabrina had brought her camera, and Cristoval had gotten a fisherman to take their picture by the lighthouse.

There were going to be a lot of good memories about this trip, Sabrina knew. She walked at Cristoval's side, her hand resting comfortably inside his.

"Let's go," Cristoval said, turning down a small, well-lit alley. "There's a little restaurant here that I know of. They serve delicious food, but they're one of the best-kept secrets in all of the marina."

"Sounds great."

"The old couple that run the place doesn't know any English," Cristoval apologized. "I hope you're okay with that."

"Sure," Sabrina said. "I'm always okay as long as I'm with you."

Cristoval squeezed her hand and stopped in the middle of the alley. "There's something I've been wanting to do for days," he said.

Sabrina's heart beat a little faster when he took her into his arms.

He held her for a moment, hesitating, then his head came down toward hers.

Before they kissed, the feeling of being watched suddenly slammed into Sabrina. She knew instantly that they weren't alone in the alley anymore.

Running feet slapped against the pavement, and a powerful light dawned on the wall to their left.

Sabrina and Cristoval turned their heads toward the running feet and the light, and away from the kiss that had almost happened.

The bright illumination made it hard to see the troll-like figures that ran for them. Gibbering voices echoed in the alley, drowning out the music coming from the restaurants and taverns at either end of the alley.

Cristoval shoved Sabrina behind him protectively, but she tripped over a loose stone in the pavement and fell. She stared at the burning pool of light on the opposite alley wall just as the old hawk-faced man stepped out of it.

Sabrina tried to get to her feet, but the man pointed his spear at her. Then she felt as though an invisible cage had fallen around her.

"Sabrina!" Cristoval fought against the troll-like things that grabbed him, but he was no match for them. "Sabrina! Are you all ri—"

The troll-like things yanked him into the pool of light and he disappeared.

The hawk-faced man walked over to Sabrina and stared down at her.

Sabrina tried to move, but whatever spell the old man had hit her with remained in effect.

"You lose, witch!" the old man cackled. "You lose and Xhalchiat loses with you!" Without another word, he turned and walked back into the pool of light on the building wall.

"Cristoval!" Sabrina yelled. "Cristoval!"

Only the old man's cackling answered her.

She struggled to get up, but the spell that held her didn't fade until the light disappeared from the wall. Standing finally, knowing it was too late to attempt to go through the wall after Cristoval, Sabrina put both hands against the solid brick and stared at the geometric symbol burned on the wall.

Cristoval had disappeared, and this time Sabrina knew he wasn't coming back on his own.

Chapter 10

Mind whirling, Sabrina pointed herself back to her house. That would be the best place to figure out what had just happened—and what she was going to do about it. With the three-hour difference in time, it was after midnight, the witching hour.

Perfect timing, Sabrina thought, because witching was all she was going to be about for a little while. She hoped that would be enough to rescue Cristoval from wherever the old hawk-faced man had taken him. The Throckmorton's tracking bracelet felt heavy around her wrist. She knew she'd have to tell her aunts what had been going on, but she wanted to wait a moment to try to take care of things by herself. Her aunts would try to protect her first, and Sabrina had to know if there was a way to help Cristoval.

When she popped into the living room, she found the television on and Miles asleep on the sofa. His robe had fallen open to reveal that he was wearing a pair of gym shorts and a Honk if You Love Aliens T-shirt that featured one of the dome-headed, big-eyed aliens that were so prevalent in UFO mythology.

Sabrina had to chuckle. From personal experience she knew that most aliens didn't look like that. Sure, a few of them did, but not all that many.

Playing on the television was a syndicated real-life alien encounters program that Miles was especially fond of. He had a bag of microwave popcorn sitting in the crook of one arm. The other arm dangled off the sofa onto the floor.

"I'm telling ya," a gravelly voice whispered from behind the kitchenette counter, "it's better if you leave the bones in the chicken. Makes it crunchier."

"And what's going to keep the chicken leg on the bread?" Salem's voice was easily recognizable. Now that she was looking in that direction, Sabrina noticed the refrigerator door was open.

"Why, the peanut butter of course. Why do you think we put that on?"

"I was thinking, Buddy," Salem said, "that it was primarily to clog your arteries."

"No, no, no! The peanut butter is there to keep everything together."

"Including the cucumbers and strawberries?" Salem asked.

"Yep. I'm telling ya, ya don't know what good eating is till you've had one of these puppies."

"Strawberries?" Sabrina stuck her head over the

kitchenette counter and glared down at Salem and the bulldog he was talking to. They had the makings of two sandwiches spread out on plates on the floor. "We had strawberries?"

"Yikes!" Salem cried out, so startled that he leaped into the air.

"The jig is up," the bulldog growled. He was huge and brown furred and wore a spiked collar under a black-and-red smoking jacket. A blue silk patch covered his right eye.

Salem came down again in an eye blink—with his claws instinctively extended. Unfortunately, he landed on the bulldog's rump.

"Yeeee-owwwwwch!" the bulldog screamed. He bucked up like a rodeo bronc and knocked the sandwich plates flying. The clatter echoed throughout the house.

Anxiously Sabrina glanced at the doorway leading up to Morgan's room. When Morgan didn't come crashing through the door to see what was going on, Sabrina figured she was at one of the parties she regularly attended.

"Get your claws outta me, you miserable hairball!" the bulldog roared.

"Slow down!" Salem yelped.

"My ear! My ear! My ear!" the bulldog squealed.

"Watch out for the—" The resounding impact of two furry bodies slamming into the wall blotted out whatever else Salem had been about to say.

Sabrina glanced back over the counter and saw Salem and Buddy stretched out on the floor. Both familiars moaned pathetically on the tiled floor, which now looked like a battlefield between tossed salads and chicken legs.

"Don't Aunt Hilda and Aunt Zelda have any food in their refrigerator?" Sabrina asked. Raiding the fridge, even one he had to travel to, was no big deal for Salem, but bringing a friend? More for Salem was, well, *more* for Salem.

"No, I mean yes," Salem said defensively. "We were just—"

The bulldog growled. "They're on diets. Bo-ring." He squinted his only eye and bared his teeth.

"Well," Sabrina said to Salem, "I like your friend's honesty, but I can't say much about his attitude." She pointed at the bulldog and put him in a doggie strait-jacket.

The bulldog looked down at the thick canvas material binding him. "Okay," he sighed tiredly, "I gotta remember this. Note to self: no more lipping off to human witches."

"By the way, you don't have any strawberries," Salem said. "You may want to put that on your shopping list."

"But I heard you say strawberries," Sabrina insisted.

"Buddy swiped those—I mean, brought those with him," Salem said.

The bulldog growled and shook his head.

"From where?" Sabrina asked suspiciously.

"The last house we went to," Salem stated matter-of-factly.

"The last house?" Sabrina repeated.

Salem explained. "It's spring break. Do you know how much food college students leave in their refrigerators when they leave town? Think of it as a public service. Sort of an impromptu food rescue plan. You know, take from those who really don't want it to turn green and hairy in their refrigerators while they're out of town, and give to those who are willing to sacrifice their waistlines to take care of the excess food. It's a win-win situation."

Just then Sabrina heard Miles yawn. When she turned, he was sitting up on the couch, blinking sleepily at her. "Hey, Sabrina. What are you doing here? Miss the boat?"

"No," Sabrina said, crossing the room to Miles. "You're having a dream. This is all a dream."

Miles ran his fingers through his hair and yawned. "Okay." He lay back down and closed his eyes.

"What are you doing?" Sabrina asked.

"I'm going back to sleep."

"You can't do that."

Miles looked puzzled. "Why not? It's my dream."

"Because I need you to answer a question for me."

"Man," Miles said, yawning, "this has to be the strangest dream I've ever had. Usually I'm the guy asking all the questions, and the FBI and the air force won't give me the answers." He yawned again. "Okay, what's your question?"

Sabrina took a folded piece of paper from her handbag. Before she'd left the alley where Cristoval had disappeared, she'd pointed up a pad of paper and some charcoal to make a rubbing of the symbol burned into the brick wall. She showed it to Miles.

"I need to know what this is," she said.

The rubbing grabbed Miles's attention. "Well, for starters, it looks Toltec. I'll have to check the Internet for this."

"Do it," Sabrina said.

Miles put his hands up in the air before him expectantly, positioned as though he were at a computer keyboard.

"What are you doing?" Sabrina asked.

"Waiting for my computer to appear," Miles explained. "It always appears in my dreams. Kind of like I'm attached to it or something."

Sabrina took him by the arm and pulled him to his feet. "Okay, tonight's dream is old-fashioned. You have to walk to the computer."

"Can't."

"Can't?" Sabrina repeated, getting totally exasperated. *Who knows what that old hawk-faced man is doing to Cristoval?*

"Nope," Miles said. "My room's a pit. I'm going to clean it up tomorrow. You're not going to see it tonight. Dream or no dream, I've got my pride. And then there's all that embarrassment to think about." He lay back down on the sofa.

"Okay, then tonight your computer will come to you." Sabrina pointed in the direction of Miles's room.

Lumbering steps sounded from Miles's room. Sabrina figured if Salem and Buddy's fight didn't wake anyone, neither would the computer.

Not even if the computer had suddenly sprouted legs and walked into the living room area, which it did.

"Cool," Miles said in wide-eyed surprise. "It's never done that before."

"Fine," Sabrina said. "Let's be wowed later. For now let's find out what we can about this symbol."

Miles nodded and looked at the computer on legs standing expectantly before him. "Can it talk?"

"Has it ever talked before?" Sabrina asked. "In your dreams, I mean."

"No, but it's never walked either. I was just thinking maybe if it could walk, maybe it could talk."

Sabrina pointed. "Sure. Tonight it can talk."

"Hello," the computer said in a man's baritone.

"That's strange," Miles said. "I've always thought of my computer as female for some reason."

Sabrina pointed again.

"Hello, Miles," the computer said in its new feminine contralto. "Let's get to work, shall we?"

"Sure," Miles said, smiling. He looked up at Sabrina. "You know, I'm going to have to have you in my dreams more often. This is totally cool."

"Yeah," Sabrina said. "I'm looking forward to it myself."

Miles quickly typed his password and began surfing the Internet. Most of the sites he hit had *conspiracy* somewhere in their address.

Sabrina paced the floor anxiously as Miles searched

the databases he had access to. Some of them were even on government sites. She tried desperately not to think what might be happening to Cristoval.

She'd thought about going to her aunts first, but it had made more sense to go to Miles. After all, he and Cristoval shared similar interests in myths and legends, and Miles would probably identify the geometric symbol faster than Hilda or Zelda. Not to sell Zelda short, but myths and legends weren't exactly the stuff science was made of. At least, not science in the Mortal Realm. The Other Realm had branches of science that could only be marveled at.

"Found it," Miles announced.

"What is it?" Sabrina peered over Miles's shoulder at the computer screen.

"It's from a legend about Xhalchiat," the computer announced. "Xhalchiat was supposed to be an ancient Toltec kingdom, though little has been found to mark its existence."

"Where can I find it?" Sabrina asked.

"I don't know," the computer admitted. "I've checked all the Web sites available to me, and none can list a definite location. However, there is some indication—through myths and fables only—that Xhalchiat used to be located near what is now known as Puerto Vallarta, Mexico."

"Xhalchiat *used* to be located there?" Sabrina asked.

"Hey," Miles objected, "I thought I was doing the computer work here."

"You are," Sabrina replied. "If it weren't for you, I couldn't do this."

"Oh. Okay." Miles frowned. "This is a really weird dream."

"Xhalchiat doesn't exist?" Sabrina asked.

"Not in this world," the computer answered. "There is some conjecture that Xhalchiat actually existed on another space-time continuum—in another dimension."

Another dimension? Cristoval was researching inter-dimensional travel!

"What else can you tell me about Xhalchiat?" Sabrina asked.

"It was reportedly a land of great beauty and prosperity," the computer replied. "The kings descended from one great royal family that had the power to keep the land and people healthy. They also had the power to keep the land secret from any would-be invaders. However, there was some inner-family fighting, and Xhalchiat's demise is attributed to King Jasil's brother, Xipe-Topec, who usurped control of the land by banishing his brother and his brother's family from the land."

Bingo! Sabrina thought. She glanced back at Miles and saw that he was asleep on the couch again. She quickly pointed the computer back to his room, then cleaned up the mess Salem and Buddy had made in the kitchen with another point. That way Miles wouldn't take the blame for it when Morgan came home.

Sabrina even cleaned up the popcorn Miles had spilled while sleeping on the couch. Then she popped Salem, Buddy, and herself over to her aunts' house.

* * *

"You're right, Sabrina," Zelda said, looking at the thick sheaf of papers that kept popping up in the toaster in the Spellman kitchen. "Xhalchiat was once a magical land in the Other Realm. It disappeared thousands of years ago."

Sabrina paused in her pacing of the kitchen floor. "Magical lands can do that?"

Hilda shrugged. "Of course they can. They're magical. That's why they're called magical lands."

"But what about the people living on them?" Sabrina asked.

"Sometimes they move," Hilda said.

Zelda looked at Salem, who lay on the kitchen counter in his customary spot. Freed from his straitjacket, Buddy the bulldog sat contritely on the floor at the foot of the counter.

"And sometimes the magical lands are abandoned because an unfavorable ruler takes them over," Zelda said.

Sabrina marveled at her aunts. Although she hadn't used the Throckmorton's tracking bracelet and had taken chances to help Cristoval, they were still concerned about helping her to help Cristoval. They hadn't been exactly happy, of course, and Sabrina knew she hadn't heard the last of the matter.

"Well, don't look at me," Salem complained. "I've never heard of Xhalchiat until today." He squinted at the clock. "It is day, isn't it? Yes, I see that it is. It's time for this cat to get his beauty sleep." He started to get up from the counter.

"You're not going anywhere," Sabrina said. "You're in big trouble for breaking into my house."

"I thought I explained that," Salem pointed out.

"No, you didn't,"

Salem sat. "Okay, I guess maybe I didn't."

Sabrina thought furiously. "Wait. You are going somewhere. Back to Mexico with me. You and your buddy, Buddy, are going to help me rescue Cristoval."

"Give me a break," Salem complained. "All we did was save you the trouble of throwing out a few limp vegetables and a couple of pieces of dried-out meat."

"Fine," Sabrina replied. "I'll just take out an ad in the Other Realm promoting your scaredy-cat service. Not only are you not safe, neither is the food in your fridge."

Salem's eyes popped open wide. He looked at Zelda. "A little help here, please?"

Zelda folded her arms, spoke to Sabrina, but the entire time stared down the cat. "I think that's a great idea, Sabrina. And can you imagine what the Witches' Council will make of Salem and Buddy's midnight raids? A few more years as a cat, possibly?"

"They wouldn't do that!"

"They might," Hilda added. "If three witches that I know very well were to decide to mention all the other things you've been guilty of the last few years."

"That's blackmail!" Salem cried.

"I know," Zelda confided, "and it's the most effective bargaining tool I've got."

"Is there any way we can get into Xhalchiat?" Sabrina asked.

Zelda looked through all her notes, adding the new ones that had just come through the toaster. "There's an addendum here suggesting that any magical land that has disincorporated or dissolved but remains hidden from casual view within the Other Realm can be accessed by members of families that once lived there. No one else will be allowed entrance."

"So there's a chance?" Sabrina asked.

Zelda nodded. "If Cristoval's family is from there, there's a really good chance. But you need someone from his immediate family."

"There's his father, Captain Sanchez," Sabrina mused. "I know he would help if he could."

"But he's not from Xhalchiat," Hilda said.

"See?" Salem said. "It's impossible. So why don't we all just go to bed and get some sleep. I'm sure Cristoval will be back by morning. Then how will you explain the cat and dog? Nope. Best that Buddy and I stay right here." He stood, stretched, and rolled his pink tongue out in a big yawn.

Sabrina pointed at the cat threateningly.

Salem flattened his ears and frowned, but he sat once more.

"Actually, we might be able to use Captain Sanchez to get into Xhalchiat," Zelda said. "If I do a reverse of the spell that's included in these notes, I think we just might be able to do it. But we'll need Captain Sanchez's permission."

"I don't think that will be a problem," Sabrina said. "Captain Sanchez is already worried about Cristoval.

He's probably going out of his mind wondering where Cristoval is. We were supposed to meet him for dinner over an hour ago." She paused her pacing again. "What I don't understand is why Xipe-Topec wants Cristoval."

Zelda flipped through her notes again. "This file isn't very well organized, and I'm not going to accept the excuse anymore that it's all because of our toaster." She ran her finger down one of the pages. "Here it is."

"Hurry. What does it say?" Sabrina asked. She needed to go after Cristoval *now!*

"This just goes to show you how haphazard the records department was five thousand years ago, when all of this happened," Zelda said. "According to these records, Xipe-Topec was brother to the king in those days."

"That's what Miles said," Sabrina interrupted.

Zelda continued. "Xipe-Topec got very jealous of his brother's power and raised an army of trolls from a nearby land within the Other Realm. The trolls forced then King Jasil and his supporters from Xhalchiat into the Mortal Realm."

"Those *were* trolls that I saw," Sabrina said.

Zelda nodded and kept on reading. "In a matter of months Xipe-Topec reportedly fell out of favor with the people that remained in the land."

"I'll guess that made him a real fun guy at parties," Hilda said.

"The people tried to stage a rebellion against Xipe-Topec, but it failed," Zelda said.

"Rebellions are really more tricky than you think,"

Salem commented. "Most people don't appreciate the effort that goes into a good rebellion."

All three witches ignored him.

"Try keeping your yap closed, cat," Buddy growled. "Maybe if they ignore us long enough, we can take it on the lam."

"And go where?" Salem asked. "Your place?"

The bulldog glared up at Salem with his one good eye. "You got something against my place, cat?"

"Oh, be quiet, you two," Zelda ordered, "or I'll turn you both into a two-headed Chihuahua."

Salem and Buddy immediately shut up.

"Xipe-Topec stopped the rebellion," Zelda said.

"Are we getting anywhere close to the reason why Xipe-Topec kidnapped Cristoval?" Sabrina asked.

Hilda shrugged. "If a vanishing magical land is involved, there's only one reason I can think of. Whoever kidnapped Cristoval is trying to keep the land for themselves. He or she or they will use Cristoval to make a binding spell and keep it hidden away."

"This is all about real estate?" Sabrina asked in disbelief.

"If a magical land suddenly reappeared in the Other Realm," Hilda said, "there are a lot of aggressive nations that might try to take it over. Instances like that keep your father busy. This is a very big deal."

"But why did Xipe-Topec have to take Cristoval?"

"Cristoval must be a member of the original ruling family," Hilda said. "That's why his mother taught him all those stories about Xhalchiat. The ruling family must have known that Xipe-Topec wouldn't be able to keep Xhalchiat hidden from them forever."

Realization dawned within Sabrina. "Do you really believe that Cristoval is a member of that ruling family?"

"Hilda's right," Zelda said. "Cristoval has to be. It's my guess that Cristoval is Xhalchiat's missing crown prince. As crown prince of the land, Cristoval would be tied more tightly to the magic that makes up that land than anyone else. And *that* has to be the reason Xipe-Topec kidnapped him. He'll probably put a sleeping spell on Cristoval, then drain his magic from him to better control the land."

Sabrina was stunned. She couldn't believe it. She had been dating a prince. Cool.

"Sabrina."

Coming out of her daze, Sabrina glanced at Hilda.

"We probably don't have much time," her aunt said.

"And a cat and mangy mutt won't really be of much help, will they?" Salem asked hopefully.

Zelda said, "Once Xipe-Topec gets Cristoval under his power, he'll start trying to seal off Xhalchiat from the outside world, including the Other Realm. If he succeeds, we won't be able to get in without a major concession from the Witches' Council."

"But they would grant it if we're too late, right?" Sabrina asked hopefully. *How late does it have to be before it's too late?* She knew that time flowed differently in the Other Realm. Which probably meant that time flowed differently in Xhalchiat. *How much time has already passed there?*

Zelda nodded. "Eventually, yes. But, Sabrina, that could take years."

"We don't have years," Sabrina said morosely. "It might already be too late!"

Chapter 11

"You expect me to believe that you're a witch?"

Standing in Captain Sanchez's quarters aboard the *Pacific Sunset,* Sabrina nodded.

Captain Sanchez sat behind a small, efficient desk in his office, which was right outside his personal quarters. Usually he was totally in control, Sabrina guessed, but at the moment he looked utterly amazed. His eyes were wide and glassy. "I'm supposed to believe this? Just as I am supposed to believe my son was taken by goblins—"

"Trolls," Salem spoke up.

The captain gazed at the black cat, then back at Sabrina. "Your cat talks?"

"All the time," Sabrina assured him.

"And that's telling the truth," Buddy said. "Only time that stupid cat keeps his mouth shut is when you pop a couple of goose-egg-size knots across that fat head of his."

"And the dog?" Captain Sanchez asked. "Both of these animals are yours?"

"Only the cat," Sabrina said quickly. "The dog is a friend of the cat." She took a deep breath and watched Captain Sanchez, wondering what Cristoval's father would say now.

She felt a little better that Hilda and Zelda were in the room with her, and Salem, too. He had decided to be a brave bodycat in the end and had insisted on coming with them. Buddy had come along for the ride. Together they had popped aboard the luxury cruiser from Westbridge only a few moments earlier. *How can Captain Sanchez remain so calm with Cristoval missing?* Sabrina felt as though she would explode with each newly drawn breath.

"You say this man, Xipe-Topec, is the one who has Cristoval?" Captain Sanchez asked.

Sabrina realized that Cristoval's father—despite his surprise and alarm—had no other way to deal with the situation but calmly. "Yes," she said.

"And you say that Xhalchiat, the land Cristoval's mother had always talked of, is real?"

"Yes," Sabrina replied. "I've been there." She decided not to tell the captain that while she'd been there she and Cristoval had been eaten by a monster in the river.

Captain Sanchez stood up behind his desk and reached for his jacket. "My wife, Cristoval's mother, used to tell me that I kept my mind closed to a great many things. She said that I had never trained myself to accept and that I was always a doubter first." He pulled his jacket on. "Tonight I choose to believe." He glanced at Sabrina. "Show me this alley where Cristoval disappeared."

Sabrina stood beside Captain Sanchez as they studied the geometric design burned into the alley wall.

"Do you believe this spell will work?" the captain asked softly.

"It's my spell," Zelda replied. "I'm really good at that sort of thing."

"And if it doesn't work?"

Sabrina shook her head and tried very hard not to think about that prospect. "It's got to work. I care about Cristoval." *I don't know what I'm going to do if it doesn't work.*

"Do you care enough, though?" Captain Sanchez asked, but the question didn't really seem to be directed at Sabrina.

"I think we're ready," Zelda said. "Captain Sanchez?"

"Please continue, señora. I stand ready and will not fail you. My thoughts are only of my son and his welfare. Even without your prompting." The captain kept his gaze fixed on the geometric symbol.

"Of course they are," Zelda soothed.

Sabrina took a deep breath and concentrated on the symbol as well. At either end of the alley she could hear throbbing music and laughing voices. It was party time in Puerto Vallarta.

As Zelda chanted her spell, Sabrina stuck her hand out, imagining that it was sliding into Cristoval's hand. She worked so hard to remember how it felt to hold hands with him that she could have sworn she felt his hand in hers then.

> *Unbar the gate,*
> *Unlock the door.*
> *Don't let these worlds stand apart*
> *One moment more.*

At first Sabrina didn't think the spell was going to work. She felt Cristoval's hand turn cold in hers, as if the feeling was being drained away from her. She hung onto it more fiercely as she thought about him. There were still so many unanswered questions that remained between them.

Then, incredibly, a small dot of light materialized in the center of the geometric pattern.

Sabrina heard Captain Sanchez's sharp intake of breath at her side.

The dot held its size for a moment, swirling around the symbol slightly as if trying to avoid the magic contained in the spell. Then the wall suddenly blazed bright with light.

"Go," Zelda said.

Without hesitation Sabrina stepped into the light and passed through the wall. Captain Sanchez was at her side. Hilda and Zelda were right behind, herding Salem and Buddy ahead of them.

As soon as she was on the other side of the magic portal, Sabrina saw immediately that she was in the same jungle as when she'd disappeared with Cristoval on the plane. They stood higher on a hill under the impossibly tall trees, but the same slow river wound through the jungle below.

Her magic now worked in Xhalchiat, Sabrina discovered when she pointed up some safari clothes for herself. She glanced at Captain Sanchez's uniform. "I can whip you up something a little more comfortable if you want."

The captain bowed his head. "No. I've worn a uniform like this for years, señorita. I shall be quite comfortable. Thank you for your concern."

Hilda and Zelda pointed up their own clothing, then Zelda pointed up a speedboat. Sabrina had already briefed her on the huge monster in the river.

Salem glanced around. "The jungle? No, not the jungle! It always has to be the jungle!" he cried plaintively.

"Quit your bellering," Buddy whispered to the cat hoarsely. "You're embarrassing me. I got a rep as a tough guy, see? And I ain't going to have you messing it up."

"Okay," Zelda called out as she headed for the speedboat, "all aboard."

Sabrina joined Zelda down in the speedboat.

"Captain," Zelda offered generously, pointing to the pilot station of the speedboat, "if you'd care to do the honors."

"Of course, señora." Captain Sanchez took the controls and soon had the speedboat racing downriver. The engines echoed loudly in the trees, scaring off huge flocks of multicolored birds.

"I guess sneaking up on Xipe-Topec isn't an option," Sabrina shouted over the roaring engines.

Zelda shook her head. "Not when so much is riding on this. We don't have time for subtlety."

"And if Xipe-Topec's magic is stronger than ours?"

Zelda hesitated.

"Then we're doomed," Hilda said.

"Oh, no!" Salem wailed. "I knew it! I knew we were going to be doomed!" He sat in the back of the speedboat with Buddy, who had discovered suddenly that his stomach didn't agree with traveling by boat. The bulldog hung his head over the side and moaned almost as loudly as the cat.

"Well," Sabrina said, "I'd say our side might not be at their perky best."

"Do you remember anything of the legends that Cristoval's mother told you about this place?" Zelda asked Captain Sanchez.

"She told me," the captain stated, "that my son is to be king of this land. She said that Xipe-Topec had driven her family and others out of Xhalchiat when he raised the rebellion against King Jasil. Many generations had passed since that had happened, but she said that from her interpretation of all the old lessons, Cristoval would be the first of the family to step back into this land."

"Her parents never mentioned any of this to you?" Sabrina asked.

"No, señorita. They joined in a telling of some of the old stories, but they never appeared to give them much credence. My wife said she had traced the tangled ancestry back to King Jasil's lineage and found that it would be she who gave birth to the potential king of Xhalchiat."

"Potential king?" Hilda asked.

"That was what scared Cristoval's mother," Captain Sanchez said. "She knew that Xipe-Topec would be aware of Cristoval's birth. The spell that he had enchanted Xhalchiat with would not last forever."

"It was supposed to give out the year Cristoval turned nineteen," Sabrina said, understanding.

"Exactly," Captain Sanchez agreed. "She always warned me to keep him close to me during his nineteenth year if something happened to her. But Cristoval, he is a young man now. When he decided to get his education, I could not stop him."

"So when Cristoval was disappearing earlier this week," Sabrina said, "that was Xipe-Topec trying to pull him over into this world?"

"I would think so," Zelda said.

"Then why was Xipe-Topec watching me?"

Captain Sanchez looked at her. "Because you are the one Xipe-Topec fears most."

"Me?" Sabrina echoed. "Why me?"

"Xipe-Topec wanted to keep you away from Cristoval," the captain said.

"I don't understand why he would go to such lengths."

"Because according to the tales Cristoval's mother told me, you are the one who has the power to wake the sleeping prince."

* * *

Only a few minutes later, the river passed under the shadow of a tall Toltec-style temple sitting high in the mountains. Sabrina gazed up the mountain, her eyes following the winding trail that led up to the temple.

Captain Sanchez nosed the speedboat in close to the riverbank. Once he had it steady, they quickly disembarked and headed up the trail.

We're being watched, Sabrina knew. By then she was very familiar with the sensation. She was really surprised that Xipe-Topec didn't send a horde of trolls to attack them.

Without warning, the sky darkened, lightning flashed, and thunder boomed across the mountains. A sudden deluge hammered them with fat raindrops that stung when they hit. A chill wind coiled through them. In seconds the winding mountain trail became a river of mud that made their footing tricky. Their pace slowed to a grinding movement.

Halfway up the mountain, winged trolls leaped from ledges and glided down toward Sabrina and the rescue party. Sabrina ducked and avoided the rocks thrown by the trolls, but it was hard to move in the loose mud. One misstep in the wrong direction would send her plunging over the mountainside.

However, the mud also had its uses.

As another troll flew toward her, Sabrina pointed at the mud. Immediately, a great pie-shaped chunk of it lifted from the mountainside and *splotzed* the troll.

"Woo-hoo!" Sabrina cried out enthusiastically.

Covered in mud, the troll squealed and fell from the

sky. The creature slammed against the mountainside all the way down to the river's edge, where it lay dazed.

"Sabrina!" Hilda cried. "That's a great idea!"

Almost instantly, mud-pie missiles filled the air and swatted down flying trolls. They screamed and bleated as they desperately tried to avoid getting *splotzed,* but the accuracy of the three witches was too much.

The flying trolls retreated, leaving the mountainside trail a little easier to climb.

Long minutes later, while the storm still raged above them, Sabrina was a mud-covered mess when she reached the outer courtyard of the temple. She felt incredibly tired, and her vision blurry from the rain and fatigue.

Flanked by dozens of trolls carrying swords and spears, the old hawk-faced man—Xipe-Topec, Sabrina assumed—stood at the mouth of a large chamber leading to the interior of the temple. He wore an angry, threatening look, and in one hand he clutched a feathered spear.

Okay, Sabrina thought frantically, *so we're outnumbered. That's all right, isn't it? After all, we* are *witches.* She glanced at her aunts and at Captain Sanchez, who didn't look dismayed at all. That was immediately heartening.

"You've come a long way just to end up as my slaves," Xipe-Topec threatened.

Captain Sanchez stepped forward bravely. His captain's whites were no longer white, but he still carried himself with dignity and grace. "We've come to get my son."

"That's going to be impossible, I'm afraid. You see, I have no intention of letting him go."

"Cristoval is the rightful heir to this land," Captain Sanchez said as he took another step forward.

Sabrina knew the captain was terribly exposed, and he didn't even have any magic to protect him. Quietly, she stepped up beside Cristoval's father.

"No," Xipe-Topec announced, "my power makes me the rightful ruler of this land. And I mean to keep it that way."

Sabrina gazed at the run-down temple. "If you've been here for five thousand years, you might have tried to do something with the place."

Xipe-Topec frowned at her. "You annoy me, girl. You have from the very beginning when you started to show interest in Cristoval. I shall enjoy breaking your spirit."

"You'll never do that," Sabrina promised.

"Once you're a slave," Xipe-Topec replied, "your first task will be to clean the royal barnyard—with a *toothbrush!*"

Sabrina thought about that. "Okay, that could be a step in the right direction to spirit-breaking."

"We're not going to be slaves," Captain Sanchez argued. "Where is my son?"

"Come," Xipe-Topec said. "I will show you." He turned and walked into a tunnel that led more deeply into the temple.

Captain Sanchez led the way, and Sabrina fell into step with him. She was immediately suspicious; Xipe-Topec didn't seem like the type to give in so easily.

This has to be a trap, she thought. Waiting for the trap to be sprung was nerve-racking.

Sabrina glanced at her aunts. From the tension showing on Hilda's and Zelda's faces, they knew it, too. Of course, they had been dealing with unscrupulous witches, warlocks, and other magic-oriented types for hundreds of years.

The tunnel branched off into different passageways. Sabrina got confused almost immediately, so out of Xipe-Topec's sight she pointed up a bag of bread crumbs and started dropping the crumbs onto the stone floor. Later, if they were in a hurry, they could follow the trail of bread crumbs out of the temple.

Unexpectedly, the passageway opened again to a large chamber. Sabrina didn't know for sure, but she guessed that they were near the center of the temple.

Xipe-Topec walked to the large throne on the left side of the chamber. He pointed to the right side of the chamber. "There is your son, Captain Sanchez."

Turning, Sabrina surveyed the right side of the room. Her heart almost stopped.

Cristoval lay on a stone platform that floated above a sunken circular area. He was dressed like a Toltec warrior in a breechcloth and gold and stone jewelry. His arms and legs were marked with red, black, yellow, and blue geometric shapes.

"What's wrong with him?" Sabrina asked.

"He's under a sleep spell," Hilda said. "Don't worry. It's going to be all right. We're going to make it all right."

"You're going to do nothing!" Xipe-Topec bellowed

from the large throne. "You're all too late to do anything! The boy is mine! His power is mine! And this land will be mine forever because he is the last of his line! It has taken me thousands of years to track down my brother's family! But now I have the last remaining heir to this land!"

"No," Captain Sanchez said sternly. "You're not keeping my son. He'll be going home with me, where he belongs." He strode toward the pit.

Even as the captain reached the edge of the sunken area, the temple began to shake. Suddenly, many of the stone tiles that made up the sunken area under the floating platform that held Cristoval dropped down, revealing a huge pit. Rocks and mortar tumbled from the ceiling overhead and fell into the pit, smashing against spikes that were revealed in the flickering light of torches mounted on the walls.

Despite the danger, Captain Sanchez stepped onto one of the floating tiles. It immediately shattered, and the captain barely kept himself from falling into the deadly pit.

"I'm keeping him," Xipe-Topec stated. "Once your son is sealed into that pit, I'll have access to all the power I'll ever need. He'll sleep forever and I'll rule forever."

Captain Sanchez wheeled on the evil sorcerer. "I'm not going to let you get away with this."

"I'm afraid there's nothing you can do about it, mortal," Xipe-Topec taunted.

Well, there's something I can do about it, Sabrina thought, remembering what Captain Sanchez had told her and why Xipe-Topec had been spying on her since she had met Cristoval at John Adams College.

The chamber continued to shake, and it seemed as though the ceiling over the pit and Cristoval would collapse at any moment. Sabrina pushed her fear out of her mind and ran toward the pit.

Xipe-Topec stood up from the throne, looking fearful and angry. He pointed his feathered spear at her. "Get the girl! Don't let her near that boy!"

Sabrina heard the flutter of troll wings behind her. She kept running, concentrating on Cristoval, knowing that if their roles had been reversed, he would have come for her. That was what Xipe-Topec feared. The feelings they had for each other were strong. Sabrina didn't know how strong they were, or what form they would finally take, but she knew she couldn't leave Cristoval in the old sorcerer's hands.

Captain Sanchez grabbed the lead flying troll bearing down on Sabrina. He knocked the troll down and took the sword it carried. Lifting the sword with sure knowledge and a swift hand, the captain fought to protect Sabrina's back.

"Hurry!" Captain Sanchez urged. "There are too many trolls to hold off for long!"

Sabrina halted at the edge of the pit and looked at the spikes beneath the remaining floating tiles. *One wrong step,* she thought, *and it's Acupuncture City.* She glanced over her shoulder and saw that Zelda and Hilda had also picked up weapons to combat the army of flying trolls.

The temple continued to shake and threatened to collapse.

"Sabrina!" Salem skidded to a stop at Sabrina's feet and peered into the spike-filled pit. "You can't try to get across those floating tiles! You'll never make it!"

"I've got to!" Sabrina studied the floating tiles, trying to figure out which ones would provide the trail to Cristoval. There had to be a way to reach him. If there wasn't a secret path, then all of the tiles would have fallen into the pit from the beginning. She knew that much about magical traps.

"Wait!" Salem gathered himself at the pit's edge. "Let me go first."

"You?"

"Me," Salem agreed unhappily. "I'm a cat and I'm fast. Besides, I promised you that I would be your bodycat."

"That might just work," Sabrina said. Hearing Buddy growl ferociously, Sabrina glanced over her shoulder and saw that the attacking trolls were slowly driving her aunts, Captain Sanchez, and Buddy back toward the edge of the pit. In another few minutes, they would be pushed onto the spikes. Or they would have to zap back home to Westbridge, and it would be too late to save Cristoval. She turned back to Salem. "Okay, let's go."

Salem shook his paws nervously. "Okay, okay! Try not to be so pushy."

"Either go or I'm going without you," Sabrina said. "The trolls aren't giving us any time."

"Yeeee-ahhhhhh!" Salem yelled as he threw himself

toward the first floating tile. He leapfrogged across the tiles, using all his feline speed and skill. Some of the tiles shattered beneath him, and he narrowly avoided falling onto the spikes, screeching out in terror each time. In a matter of heartbeats, though, his leaping and bounding had revealed the trail of floating tiles that led to Cristoval.

Without hesitation, Sabrina leaped onto the first tile and quickly made her way to the floating platform where Cristoval lay sleeping. She looked down at him as the chamber shook again, dropping even more rocks and mortar around them.

I hope this works, Sabrina thought. She remembered all the dates she'd had with Cristoval during the last week, and the kiss they had almost shared in the alley before Xipe-Topec and his flying trolls arrived. When Captain Sanchez had explained to her what she had to do to break the evil sorcerer's sleeping spell, she hadn't believed it at first.

Stuff like that only happened in fairy tales.

But Sabrina believed in fairy tales. After all, somewhere in the Other Realm, they were all true.

She leaned down and kissed Cristoval.

Almost immediately, Cristoval opened his hazel eyes and looked up at her. He smiled. "Hey," he said sleepily, "I was just thinking about you."

The chamber shook again and more rocks tumbled down. Some of them smashed onto the floating platform, rocking it like a ship on rough seas.

Quickly, Cristoval got to his feet and helped Sabrina

to hers. He glanced around the temple chamber and lifted a hand.

Sabrina could feel the magic working in Cristoval now. It was stronger than anything she'd ever witnessed in her life.

"Enough," Cristoval said.

Immediately, the trolls backed down and stopped fighting.

Xipe-Topec, however, wasn't finished. He rushed toward the pit's edge, screaming and shaking his spear. That was when Buddy the bulldog latched onto the evil sorcerer from behind and stopped Xipe-Topec in his tracks.

"I got a suggestion for you, chump," Buddy said in a muffled voice. "Come along quietly."

Xipe-Topec dropped his spear and did as the bulldog suggested.

Holding hands, Sabrina and Cristoval sat near the windows in El Faro the next day. The sun had streaked the sky red and purple and gold, and the sea looked green beneath it.

"So what are you going to do about college?" Sabrina asked.

"Take some time off," Cristoval answered. "Xipe-Topec did a lot of bad things to my mother's land while he had control of it. They are going to take a long time to sort out and fix."

"But you can do it," Sabrina said positively.

Cristoval nodded. "I know. It's what my mother

would have wanted. And to tell the truth, it's what I want." He looked at her with those sparkling hazel eyes. "I just wish . . ."

"I know," Sabrina said, squeezing his hand. "But maybe this moment and this spring break was all we were meant to have together."

"I don't feel that way."

"Neither do I," Sabrina agreed. "But if this is all that was meant to be, I want you to know it was absolutely wonderful."

Cristoval nodded. "Well, Xhalchiat has waited for five thousand years for everything to be put back to order. Your aunts have contacted the Witches' Council regarding Xhalchiat's status in the Other Realm. I think I'm going to get to meet your dad before all of this is over." He looked more nervous about that than he had while hanging over a pit filled with deadly spikes.

"Don't worry about my dad," Sabrina said. "He's a great guy, and I think you'll like him."

"Hey," a deep, gravelly voice whispered. "You know you two talk way too much. You're wasting a perfectly good sunset out there and a decent band in here. If I were you, I'd put on my dancing shoes and make the most of the evening."

Sabrina and Cristoval looked at the neighboring table. Salem and Buddy were perched on chairs and wolfing down one of everything on the menu. It had been Sabrina's payment for their help in rescuing Cristoval.

"Why, Buddy," Sabrina said in surprise, "you don't

come across as someone who would have a romantic bone in his body."

Buddy looked around furtively and held up a paw. Sabrina hadn't known until that time that bulldogs could look sheepish.

"Hey, now! Easy with that kind of chatter. I got a reputation to think of." The bulldog looked at Sabrina and winked his good eye. "Just so you know, I like my romantic bones extra crunchy."

"That sun's not going to wait for you," Salem pointed out. "It's going down . . . now."

Cristoval stood and offered Sabrina his hand. "Would you care to dance, milady?" he asked her in a properly princely fashion.

"I'd love to." Sabrina followed him out onto the dance floor and allowed herself to be pulled into his arms. And they danced as the sea drank down the sun, neither of them thinking about tomorrow but living only for the moment.

About the Author

Mel Odom lives in Moore, Oklahoma, with his wife and five children. Besides books in the *Sabrina, the Teenage Witch* series, he's also written for *Buffy the Vampire Slayer* and *Angel*. He usually cruises the Other Realm, too, but through the Internet. You can reach him at mel@melodom.net.

**A fun-filled guide
to the mystery and
magic of the universe!**

Sabrina's Guide
to the Universe

Using my magic, Salem and I traveled
through outer space and now we want
to share our discoveries with you!

by
Patricia Barnes-Svarney

**From Archway Paperbacks
Published by Pocket Books**

BASED ON THE HIT TV SERIES

Charmed™

Prue, Piper, and Phoebe Halliwell
didn't think the magical incantation
would really work. But it did.
Now Prue can move things with her
mind, Piper can freeze time, and
Phoebe can see the future. They are
the most powerful of witches—
the Charmed Ones.

**Available from Pocket Pulse
Published by Pocket Books**

2387

"I'm the Idea Girl, the one who can always think of something to do."

VIOLET EYES

A spellbinding new novel of the future

by Nicole Luiken

Angel Eastland knows she's different. It's not just her violet eyes that set her apart. She's smarter than her classmates and more athletically gifted. Her only real competition is Michael Vallant, who also has violet eyes—eyes that tell her they're connected, in a way she can't figure out.

Michael understands Angel. He knows her dreams, her nightmares, and her most secret fears. Together they begin to realize that nothing around them is what it seems. Someone is watching them, night and day. They have just one desperate chance to escape, one chance to find their true destiny, but their enemies are powerful—and will do anything to stop them.

Available from

POCKET
PULSE

Published by Pocket Books

3074

William Corlett's

THE MAGICIAN'S HOUSE QUARTET

Thirteen-year-old William Constant and his two younger sisters, Mary and Alice, have come to ancient, mysterious Golden House in Wales for the holidays. Their lives will never be the same once they enter the Magician's House—and discover their destiny.

THE STEPS UP THE CHIMNEY

THE DOOR IN THE TREE

THE TUNNEL BEHIND THE WATERFALL

THE BRIDGE IN THE CLOUDS

Available from Archway Paperbacks
Published by Pocket Books

3044-01